**"What you need to do, Miss Sutton, is leave before I call Nettleton & Thompson and tell them to fire you."**

"For what?" Rosalind snapped. Determination lent strength to her voice. Irritation added an edge. "Doing my job? Going above and beyond by tracking you down across two countries?"

"If going against your client's wishes and stalking them is considered your job, then I'll take my business elsewhere."

Silence fell, save for the furious thudding of her heart in her chest.

"Do you not understand? If you don't sign, you'll lose everything—"

"I've already lost plenty, Miss Sutton." Cold suffused his words, all traces of amusement and admiration gone. He started walking down, slow, measured steps that made her chest tighten with dreaded anticipation. "My father. My fiancée. My looks. My ability to walk in a crowd without scaring small children." The shadows crept up, revealed broad shoulders and a strong neck, the skin marred by one pinkish-colored scar. "What makes you think I give a damn about money anymore?"

# The Diamond Club

*Billion-dollar secrets behind every door...*

Welcome to The Diamond Club: the world's most exclusive society, open only to the ten richest men and women alive. The suites are opulent. The service is flawless. And privacy is paramount! You'll never see the details of these billionaires' blistering romances in any of the papers—but you can read all about them right here!

All available now!

# STRANDED AND SEDUCED

**EMMY GRAYSON**

**Harlequin**

**PRESENTS**

 **Harlequin®**
**PRESENTS™**

ISBN-13: 978-1-335-93905-0

Stranded and Seduced

Copyright © 2024 by Emmy Grayson

For questions and comments about the quality of this book, please contact us at CustomerService@Harlequin.com.

TM and ® are trademarks of Harlequin Enterprises ULC.

Harlequin Enterprises ULC
22 Adelaide St. West, 41st Floor
Toronto, Ontario M5H 4E3, Canada
www.Harlequin.com

**Printed in Lithuania**

MIX
Paper | Supporting responsible forestry
FSC® C021394

**Emmy Grayson** wrote her first book at the age of seven about a spooky ghost. Her passion for romance novels began a few years later with the discovery of a worn copy of Kathleen Woodiwiss's *A Rose in Winter* buried on her mother's bookshelf. She lives in the Midwest countryside with her husband (who's also her ex-husband), their children and enough animals to start their own zoo.

### Books by Emmy Grayson

### Harlequin Presents

*Cinderella Hired for His Revenge*
*His Assistant's New York Awakening*

### The Infamous Cabrera Brothers

*His Billion-Dollar Takeover Temptation*
*Proof of Their One Hot Night*
*A Deal for the Tycoon's Diamonds*

### The Van Ambrose Royals

*A Cinderella for the Prince's Revenge*
*The Prince's Pregnant Secretary*

### Hot Winter Escapes

*An Heir Made in Hawaii*

### Diamonds of the Rich and Famous

*Prince's Forgotten Diamond*

Visit the Author Profile page
at Harlequin.com.

To Mr. Grayson, Mom and Dad, this book would not have been finished without your support.

To my editor Charlotte, I'm a better writer because of you.

To my darling children, this book would have been finished a lot sooner if you would sleep through the night.

# CHAPTER ONE

GRIFFITH LYKAOIS TRACED a finger over the scar that cut through his right eyebrow, skimmed the corner of his eye and sliced over his cheek. Another scar stretched from the side of his mouth down to his chin, surprisingly smooth to the touch. Still a visible angry red slash even when he combed his beard to cover it. As he sat in the leather high-back chair by the balcony doors, a glass of whiskey within reach, he could picture his ghoulish visage in his mind as if he was looking in a mirror. The past eleven months had faded the scars to dull pink. But time hadn't dimmed the memory of the first time he'd seen himself. Stitches crisscrossing the fresh wounds. Eyes bloodshot and unfocused from the medication they'd pumped into him.

*Monstrous.*

Her horrified voice had slithered through him, that word burying under his skin, as he'd drifted in and out of consciousness that first day.

Not even his status as the son of a wealthy shipping magnate, with millions in the bank, had been enough to make Kacey Dupree want to stick around. Not when her boyfriend had looked more like a beast than a man.

*Surely you must understand, Griff.*

Her voice had sounded like nails on a chalkboard, digging into his brain like sharp talons as he'd tried to wrap his mind around the fact that his father had been killed and he'd been left scarred.

All because he hadn't been paying attention. Had been focused on himself, as his father had just accused him of, before the world had been tossed upside down with a bone-wrenching jolt and screeching metal.

The word echoed in his mind as he dropped his hand from his face and grabbed the glass. A sip of the whiskey, straight and tinged with spice, burned down his throat. He avoided getting drunk. Too easy of an out.

But he allowed himself just enough to dull the pain.

*Monstrous.*

Kacey had visited him the second day in the hospital, her glistening blond hair twisted into an elegant chignon that had displayed her pale, heart-shaped features perfectly. A beauty that hadn't even registered as he'd fought against pain and grief. She'd laid her hand on his shoulder, then snatched it back quickly, her plump red lips twisted into an expression of disgust when she'd seen the blood seeping through the bandage.

Rage had simmered beneath the dressings. His father had just died.

"Surely you must understand, Griff."

"Give me the necklace."

Her mouth had dropped open. She'd switched from placating to furious in seconds, raging at him for daring to take away the one thing that would leave her with memories of what they'd had before the accident. It had only been when he'd threatened to sue her for theft and ensure the news made it into the papers that she'd taken off the four-million-dollar ruby necklace and hurled it at him before rushing out in a fit of tears.

That his first thought had been *Good riddance* said more about their six-month relationship than he ever could have. It had hurt more that it hadn't hurt much at all.

With one hand still wrapped around the glass, his other came up, fingers touching the tiny moon-shaped scar on the left side of his face. The only visible injury to that side. The thin scar high on his left temple from where his head had slammed into the doorframe had been covered by hair.

But he could feel it. Feel it when he combed his hair. Feel it when it throbbed at night with a pain that felt as deep and fresh as the moment he'd heard his father shout his name before everything had turned black.

Kacey had been right about one thing. He *was* a monster. Inside and out.

He took another sip of whiskey. Aged sixty years in the wilds of Ireland, one of the hand-painted bottles fetched over one million dollars at Sotheby's New York location. A year ago, he would have been on top of the world with one of Europe's most coveted models sitting across from him, the finest jewels his money could buy around her neck, and the whiskey in his glass.

Now it was merely a means to an end. A good-tasting whiskey that eased his discomfort and helped pass the time.

Fate, he'd discovered, had a very cruel sense of humor. For the past ten years he'd been consumed by money and image. When he'd first heard of the Diamond Club four years ago, envy had been an ugly shadow dodging his steps. The clubhouse, a casual name for an opulent town house in London, offered refuge for the ten wealthiest people in the world. Rumors had spread like wildfire of the amenities: a helipad on the roof, columns fashioned from Calcutta marble and suites designed to its residents' particular tastes.

Now, as he stood and walked through the suite his father had had decorated, he no longer felt envy.

He just felt sick.

Three months after the accident, when his spinal fractures had been declared healed enough for him to remove the back brace, a lawyer had visited him at the family estate in Kent. His father had branched out over the past few years, investing in everything from real estate to technology. Those investments had resulted in a fortune worth billions.

Enough billions that the lawyer's visit had been shortly followed by an invitation. The cream-colored envelope had been delivered by a woman in a black suit that matched the limo she arrived in. She had inclined her head and handed him the envelope as she told him Mr. Raj Belanger cordially invited him to take his father's place at the Diamond Club.

Once one of his loftiest goals, now achieved. At the expense of his father's life.

Yes. Fate was very, very cruel.

He hadn't been able to bring himself to leave the safety of Kent, the familiarity of the gleaming wood floors, the antique furniture he'd once scoffed at. Now he understood his father's inability to get rid of the chesterfield sofa with its worn arms where he'd once sat with his mother as they watched old movies. His refusal to sell the faded Persian rug in front of the fireplace where Griffith had sat in the winter and opened Christmas presents.

Too late, he saw the value, saw the wisdom of his father's words, understood the caution urged upon him not to get too caught up in opulence and bank statements.

With both his parents gone now, the pieces of furniture were no longer old heirlooms he wanted to replace, the home no longer old and lacking the polish he preferred in his purchases. Now the sofas and rugs and chairs inspired memories of times he could never get back. The home welcomed him with open arms, despite all the disparaging remarks he'd made.

Much as his parents had.

Kent had become a harbor, a place to hide. The familiarity of his surroundings, the warmth of a place he'd once called home, had given him the kind of solace none of his ritzy penthouses and expensive town houses had.

But his refuge had been ruined a week ago when he'd been out walking along the shores of the private lake and a light had flashed in the trees. The next day, a picture of him looking down at the ground had appeared on the front of a tabloid magazine. The picture had been a touch out of focus, enough to blur the worst of his scars. But it was evident that the man who had once been lauded as one of the handsomest in Europe was no longer so.

The story had included a full recounting of the car accident that had claimed the life of his father, Belen Lykaois. It had also revealed that the head of Lykaois Shipping had been worth far more than hundreds of millions of dollars. He had been worth billions.

Billions that had been left to his sole surviving heir, Griffith Lykaois.

The phone calls had started less than an hour later. The vultures had descended, including invitations to charity galas, private yacht vacations, dinner parties and of course more investments, scams, people clawing for a piece of his wealth.

Wealth he had once dreamed of. Wealth he could barely now stomach the thought of possessing.

Kacey's call had been the final straw. He'd just gotten off the phone with his secretary in London who had been fielding calls for interviews, events and the like. His private cell phone had rung, and he'd answered without checking.

Kacey had greeted him with that nickname he'd loathed—Griff—and told him she missed him and could she see him please to apologize—

He'd tossed the phone out the window into the pond below without a second thought.

Security had caught two more paparazzi later that evening. His sanctuary tainted, he'd taken his limo down to London, to the one place he knew would be as secure, if not more so, than Buckingham Palace.

The Diamond Club.

He'd walked into the lobby from a private back entrance off the mews and been greeted by a portly man with a beak-like nose and one of the most elaborate silver moustaches he'd ever seen. Lazlo, as the man had introduced himself with a deferential bow, had led him across the marbled floor of the grand hall and up a sweeping staircase. The hallway had been covered in silk carpeting that masked the sound of their footsteps as they'd walked to a black door with a gold number eight.

He'd been here for six days now, stalking around the suite like a caged animal. That Griffith's father had had it decorated not for himself, but for his son, had been obvious. Soaring windows with black trim on one side, an accent wall of red brick, and creamy-colored paint elsewhere balanced warmth with the industrial look Griffith favored. After his mother's death, he'd grown to detest the old-world charm of their estate in Kent. The style he imagined his father would have selected if he'd decorated for himself. But Belen had chosen gleaming metal and glass, the style Griffith preferred that, as Griffith had argued numerous times, signified progress.

Whenever Griffith looked around, at the leather furniture, at the original artwork on the walls, he didn't experience any pleasure. Just shame. Shame and a deep-rooted self-loathing that he had rejected everything his father stood for, kept him at arm's length for so long while Belen had continued to love him from afar. He'd even eschewed his own preferences as he decorated the Diamond Club suite for his ungrateful son.

Griffith had everything he'd talked of wanting, only to find that he was missing the one thing he'd had all along and never appreciated. The last conversation he'd had with his father, more of an argument than a discussion, had been an old one. Belen had been concerned about... well, everything. Griffith's long work hours. His relationship with Kacey. His spending.

"I don't spend your money," Griffith had snapped as he stopped at a light. "I spend the money I earn. You yourself just acknowledged I work my ass off for this company."

"And for what?" Belen retorted. "Rolex watches? Paintings and sculptures you stash away in one of your numerous penthouses?"

"You own beautiful things."

"Yes, and I enjoy them. I don't just buy them to have them. Your grandfather built Lykaois Shipping from nothing. My early years were poor. Your grandfather lived most of his life poor. To have the wealth we have now—"

"Is earned, not a right," Griffith finished. The edge in his voice widened the growing chasm between them.

Belen had sighed, a sigh that cut straight through Griffith's anger and lodged in the part of his heart that would always be a boy seeking his father's approval.

"There's more to life, son, than things."

"Things are like trophies. Evidence of success. The result of hard work." His hands tightened on the wheel. "Tangible."

Griffith shoved the memory away before he could relive what had followed. He moved to the balcony, leaned his forehead against the cool glass. Plush chairs surrounded a glass fire pit. Wrought iron fencing rose up just high enough to interrupt prying eyes from nearby buildings. Black lanterns fixed to the fencing gleamed bright as gray clouds rolled across the sky, growing darker with impending rain.

What was he going to do? Lykaois Shipping, his grandfather's pride and the legacy that had elevated their family from poverty-stricken resistance fighters in World War II to the upper echelons of the world's wealthy, was being run by an efficient team in his absence. No one had questioned his request for a yearlong sabbatical. Between his extensive injuries and his father's death, not to mention the international scrutiny, the board had vocalized complete support in the virtual meeting he'd conducted. He'd kept his camera turned off.

Not because they'd wanted to be rid of him. No, as his executive assistant had shared, they wanted him to rest so that he would come back stronger than ever. After he'd been put in charge of the British division of Lykaois Shipping five years ago, everything had soared: the company's share of container traffic, accuracy, profits. The board wanted him to do the same for the entire company. Even if they had to wait a year for him to bury his ghosts and adjust to his new reality.

Griffith stepped out onto the balcony, moved to the edge and gazed out over London, the blend of old and new. A cool wind whipped across the rooftops. A few miles away lay the London office of Lykaois Shipping. What had once energized him, given him a reason to get up in the morning, now felt hollow.

An icy-cold raindrop fell on his face. Before he could turn away, the clouds unleashed a downpour that soaked him before he could make it to the door.

*Perfect.*

He stepped inside, shaking raindrops off like a dog, just in time to hear the quiet buzz of his private line.

"Yes."

"Sir." Lazlo's voice, deep and proper, rolled through the line. "There's a young lady to see you."

If anger could manifest into something physical, steam would rise from his clothes.

"You can tell Miss Dupree that she can ride her broomstick back to wherever she came from or go straight to hell. I don't care which."

"As enjoyable as that would be, sir, it's not Miss Dupree."

Griffith frowned.

"Who is it?"

"Rosalind Sutton of Nettleton & Thompson."

The firm that had handled all of his father's estate planning. A firm that dated back over two hundred years and managed the assets, wills and trusts of CEOs, politicians, even the occasional royal. They wanted him to sign the papers that would officially transfer his father's fortune to him. This woman, Rosalind Sutton, had certainly been tenacious, from calling his private number to showing up at his various offices and even his home in Kent. Thankfully, he'd been gone that weekend. Otherwise, she might have found herself a guest of the local constabulary for the night.

He knew at some point he would have to cave. Would have to sign the damned papers and acknowledge that his father was gone.

But not today. He wasn't ready.

*You'll never be ready.*

Ignoring that nasty little voice inside his head, his next words were terse. "Tell her I'll contact her later."

"Of course, sir."

A rustling sound eclipsed Lazlo's voice.

"Miss Sutton—"

A feminine voice, strong yet muffled, replied, "Give me the phone. I need to—"

Griffith paused. He knew the voice, had heard it on the one voice mail he'd listened to before deleting it and blocking the number. Cool and professional. Yet this version of the voice was vibrant, feminine with a brash confidence that awoke something inside him.

Lazlo's exasperated voice cut through once more. "Miss Sutton—"

The line went dead.

# CHAPTER TWO

GRIFFITH STARED AT the phone. His previous irritation with Miss Sutton's inability to take no for an answer morphed, shifted into admiration for the woman who had somehow managed to get into one of the world's most exclusive clubs. The American accent hadn't even registered when he'd listened to the voice mail. Now it intrigued him, made him want to know more about the tenacious woman who worked for one of the most exclusive law firms in London.

It had been a long time since anything had interested him.

His lips quirked. Imagining Lazlo fending off a woman trying to wrestle the phone away brought him as close to a laugh as he'd gotten in nearly a year.

He returned the phone to its cradle and started for the stairs, which led to the second floor of his suite where a massive king bed waited for him. Then he stopped as curiosity warred with encroaching exhaustion.

Curiosity won.

He walked out into the main hall, the walls tastefully decorated with a mix of contemporary and classic paintings by legendary artists. Sconces provided light all the way down to the top of the grand staircase. The marble marvel swept down to the main hallway, a large room lined with columns and a soaring ceiling that boasted a tiered chandelier crafted from diamonds.

The expense and beauty were lost on the people down below. Lazlo stalked out of his office, the figure at his side mostly obscured by his broad body. He moved with purpose across the hall.

"You are not welcome here again, Miss Sutton." Lazlo's voice, usually polite and refined, dripped with icy command.

"Aren't you supposed to be serving your clients?"

The same husky, feminine voice Griffith had heard on the phone drifted up, wrapped around him with a surprisingly strong grip. He moved closer to the top of the stairs.

Lazlo turned and guided Miss Sutton toward the double front doors where two security guards waited. It gave Griffith his first glimpse of the tenacious attorney who had been badgering him these past few weeks.

His first impression was curls. A riotous mass of dark brown curls cascaded over her shoulders and down her back. She wore a tan trench coat that skimmed the back of her knees and navy rain boots.

"Yes. Mr. Lykaois doesn't want to see you."

"But if he doesn't see me, he'll risk—"

"Might I suggest calling his secretary?"

"I have. Multiple times. I've also driven to his offices in Liverpool, Portsmouth, Southampton…"

As if sensing his presence, she suddenly whipped her head around and looked up. Their eyes met. She held his gaze even as Lazlo continued to move her forward.

A current of emotion arced between them. The anticipation of two adversaries finally coming face-to-face charged the air. Yet something deeper wound its way through, added a dark, hypnotic power just before desire slammed into him. Vivid images filled his mind, carnal thoughts of a slender body arching beneath his as he tangled his fingers deep into those curls, kissed her bare throat as she curved against him——

Shaken, his hand shot out and gripped the banister, his fingers digging into the marble with such force it was a miracle he didn't leave indentations in the polished stone.

"Mr. Lykaois?"

His chest tightened as he forced himself to stay in place. He was in the shadows. She couldn't see him clearly. He couldn't even make out any defining features, aside from an oval-shaped face framed by those unruly curls. But it didn't stop the voice from slipping beneath his skin, wrapping around his taut nerves and teasing, coaxing, urging him to stay just a moment longer, to look his fill of the woman who had set his body on fire.

"Mr. Lykaois, please. I need to speak to you about your inheritance."

The last word snapped him out of his reverie. Cold flooded his veins as his hands tightened into fists at his sides. He turned his back on Rosalind Sutton and returned to his suite, ignoring the fading sound of her voice calling out his name.

With each step he took, he grabbed the errant strands of his self-control and wove them back to order. If he had thought Rosalind Sutton a mere nuisance before, one who was pushing him to accept something he didn't want to, he now saw her in a far different light. In the span of a heartbeat, lust had taken over, gripped him with a ferocity he'd never experienced before. That it transcended his previous hedonistic exploits, that just the sound of her voice had inspired him to act on impulse and go out to the lobby to get a glimpse of her face, were warning signs he couldn't afford to ignore.

He had worked hard the past eleven months to correct his lifestyle. To listen to his father's words, even if it had been too late for Belen to see the results of his tireless support and love for his only child.

Rosalind Sutton threatened it all. That he could not allow.

He stalked back into his suite and walked up the stairs, pausing on the landing to stare out the window that overlooked the street below. London was now awash in dark gray, the people below pummeled by sheets of a rain too cold for the beginnings of summer.

Just below him, an umbrella opened. It caught his eye because of the almost painfully bright yellow material. It moved amongst a sea of black and crossed the road, covering its owner from view.

He knew, even before he caught a glimpse of the navy rain boots and trench coat flapping in the rain, that Rosalind wielded the colorful parasol. The umbrella moved down the sidewalk and away from the Diamond Club at a brisk pace.

How had she managed to brazen her way into the club? Into Lazlo's private office? The woman had guts, he'd give her that.

But she also wanted him to face a reckoning. To her, it was a simple signature, one last bit of business.

To him, it would be the final acknowledgment his father was gone.

He would need to sign the papers eventually. Alone, in a location of his choosing, with Rosalind far, far away. He could not risk another face-to-face meeting with a woman who tempted him to sin with her mere presence. Angry as he was at his reaction to her, it wasn't her fault. His anger needed to be directed fully and completely at himself.

It would be easy, preferable even, to place the blame for his unnatural reaction on her. But that would also be indulging in his old ways. Not taking responsibility for himself, for his actions and the consequences incurred by his selfish nature.

He turned away, firmly dismissing her from his mind as he continued up the stairs. Eventually he would deal with the damned inheritance. But right now, he wanted peace. Needed it if he wasn't going to go mad. Kent was no longer safe. While the Diamond Club offered refuge, the longer he stayed the more his guilt pressed on him, tightening until he could barely breathe.

Yet every property he owned outside of England was the opposite of peaceful. A penthouse in New York City, a beach house in California, and an apartment in Tokyo he'd acquired weeks before the accident. Luxurious, expensive and surrounded by people.

He paused at the top of the stairs, glanced down at the sumptuous furniture laid out on the floor below him. Thinking of the beach house made him think of another beach, one he hadn't been to in over thirteen years. His heart twisted in his chest, sharp and vicious, then released as he forced the emotions away and focused on the practicality. It was certainly remote, unlikely to attract the attention of anyone who would care.

Relief eased the edges of the tension straining his body. He'd always sworn he'd never go back to the far-flung coast of Normandy, to the chateau his mother had poured her heart and soul into right before her death. But not only would it serve as the perfect hiding place, it would also be just punishment.

He walked into the bedroom, ignoring the bottle of pain pills on the nightstand as he stripped off his clothes with harsh movements that made his right arm and leg burn. Then he sank down onto the bed, closed his eyes and slept fitfully, his nightmares plagued by breaking glass, squealing tires and a yellow umbrella darting to and fro amidst the chaos.

# CHAPTER THREE

*One week later*

WHITE OAK TREES towered on both sides of the lane, their thick branches creating a canopy so thick only the smallest slivers of sunlight pierced the ground. But in those little pockets of sunshine, the crushed seashells covering the drive glowed white.

Rosalind Sutton stood and stared, one hand clutched around her briefcase, the other around her umbrella. Beyond the trees there would be a gate, and beyond the gate lay the castle.

*Not castle*, she mentally corrected herself, *chateau*.

She'd learned that from Bonar, the kind, elderly man who'd given her a ride from the village and shared his extensive knowledge of the Chateau du Bellerose as his clunky truck had sputtered along a dirt road flanked by rolling hills.

The stone bridge that separated her from the trees linked the chateau to the rest of the world. A river cut through the gorge that separated the plateau the manor had been built on, providing the only way in or out. Key, Bonar had said, to defending the manor house when it had first been built.

And now providing sanctuary for one very stubborn, very rude billionaire who had a contract to sign.

The memory of that moment in the hall of the Diamond Club crept into Rosalind's mind. She'd felt someone watching her, had taken a guess as to who spied on her just beyond the light from the diamond chandelier. She had only seen his legs, hands hanging at his side. The rest of his body had been masked by darkness.

When she'd said his name, something had arisen between them, pulsed. A jolt of energy, a shock of sensual awareness.

Awareness that had evaporated as soon as she'd said the word *inheritance*. She had felt the anger, seen his hands tighten into fists.

And known that whatever battles she had fought so far, from sitting outside of his office in the pouring rain to calling in a number of favors just to determine the address of the elusive Diamond Club, were nothing compared to the war she would have to wage to secure that signature.

Instinct, along with extensive research, had prompted her to keep tabs on the Lykaois private jet at Heathrow Airport. A flight plan had been filed the morning after she'd been escorted out of the Diamond Club. A short trip from London to Le Havre on the Normandy coast. A quick review of the Lykaois family properties in France had netted several results, including a penthouse in Paris and a villa on the shores of the French Riviera.

But there had been only one in the Normandy region: a centuries-old manor just outside of the small village of Étretat.

One train and two taxis later, she was finally here. No henchmen in Savile Row suits to toss her out. No stone-faced secretaries telling her to stop coming by unless she wanted to be arrested.

Yet still she hesitated. Part of her wanted to turn around and follow the dirt road down to Étretat. To walk through the streets lined with homes constructed of timber and brick, to relax with a glass of wine at a beachside restaurant and gaze at the white chalk cliffs. To seize a moment's peace.

*Later.* She made herself that promise as she forced herself to walk across the bridge toward the shadowy tunnel created by the trees. After securing Mr. Lykaois's signature, she would enjoy the remaining days of her cottage rental. Maybe she would even take an actual vacation, spend a week in Paris or Rome.

*Yeah, right.*

Once she secured this promotion, her already demanding schedule would become even more so. Late nights, long weekends, holidays. The price to pay for working her way up at a prestigious law firm.

She'd been working toward this promotion ever since she graduated law school and accepted a position as a junior associate at Nettleton & Thompson. Her ascension from a small town in Maine to being offered a job in London had made her parents so proud. It had been her mother's dying wish to see Rosalind reach even further, achieve even more, than anyone in her family had ever dared to dream.

Sometimes, Rosalind wondered if she should have told her parents how much she would have preferred a smaller firm, an organization dedicated to helping people who needed her services versus the ones who could pay a small fortune.

But then she remembered her last conversation with

her mother, the pride that had rang in Jane Sutton's weakening voice.

It wasn't just her version of the dream that mattered.

The next step of that dream was within reach, so close it nearly drove her mad that one man held the power over her career with Nettleton & Thompson.

Unbidden, the one glimpse she'd gotten of that man rose in her mind. Cloaked in shadow, there had been no reason for her body to respond to the glance they'd shared.

Tension tightened her muscles, her breath quickening as she remembered the sudden burst of heat deep within her belly, a heat that had spread and made her body languid even as sparks had skipped through her veins.

Utterly ridiculous.

So why couldn't she forget it? Why had she woken up every morning for the past week tangled in her sheets with her heart pounding, tendrils of sensual dreams she'd never experienced before lingering with her throughout the day?

She paused halfway across the bridge. Morbid curiosity drew her to the edge and she leaned over. The drop down to the thin line of water at the bottom of the gorge was dizzying. She sucked in a deep breath, knew she was secure behind the solid wall of stone. But her heart beat a little faster as she continued on.

On toward the one man who had stirred inside her a carnal curiosity that, despite her best intentions, she couldn't ignore.

It had been easy to resist the attentions of overly hormonal teenage boys when she'd been so fixated on earning money for college. Then, once she'd reached Chicago, dating had fallen low on her priority list. One girl in her dorm, Louisa, had accused her of having impossible standards. Of building up what her first time would be like to impossible heights no man could meet.

Perhaps, Rosalind thought as her shoes scraped across the stone underfoot, Louisa had been right. Perhaps she'd never let her dates go beyond a kiss because she'd been afraid. Afraid that her fantasies of her first time, of intimacy and sex and the man she would share her body with, would fall far short of her desires.

Except now everything she'd ever dreamed about in the safety of her own bed and her own flat was coming to life at the worst possible moment.

Not to mention the worst possible man.

Her phone rang and yanked her out of her immature thoughts. Cursing when she saw who was calling, she answered.

"Yes, sir?"

"Where are you?"

Robert Nettleton's voice, smooth as whiskey and cold as ice, snapped through the line.

"France, sir."

"Making progress, then?"

"Yes, sir."

*Kind of...sort of...not really.*

"Good. I needn't remind you of what rides on the completion of this contract, Miss Sutton."

She gritted her teeth.

*Only every other time we've talked the past six weeks.*

"No, sir."

"Good. The deadline is eight days away."

"I have a flight booked back to London for Tuesday, sir."

"Be in my office by Wednesday morning at nine a.m.

with the signed contract, Miss Sutton. I want to see it with my own eyes. Daily updates are encouraged."

She rolled her eyes. It was as if her hard work the past few years had been wiped away over one damned document.

"Yes, sir."

"Your future at this firm—"

A burst of static made her wince as she moved off the bridge and into the shadows of the trees.

"Sir?" The static faded, followed by a single beep. "Great." Rosalind shoved her phone in her pocket. While she wasn't upset at her conversation being cut short, she didn't care for the lack of reception as she prepared to walk into the proverbial lion's den.

*Walk to the chateau. Get the signature. Get out.*

Cool air kissed her skin as she moved beneath the trees. Quiet descended, save for the soft crunch of shells beneath her feet and the occasional trill of a bird. The tension she'd been carrying slowly drained away, replaced by the peace she had desperately been seeking ever since she'd had the unfortunate luck to be assigned to the Lykaois case.

The research she'd conducted on the new CEO of Lykaois Shipping, the third generation to hold that title since the company was founded, had been fascinating. Griffith Lykaois was known to indulge in pleasures most people couldn't even dream of. Six-figure bottles of wine. A contemporary painting that would have paid for two dozen students from her tiny hometown to go to college. Black truffle and caviar dinners at the most expensive restaurants in the world. And of course, as evidenced by the numerous photos taken over the years, a revolving door of glamorous women on his arm. Even when he had finally settled down for more than a week with one woman, it had been a supermodel famous for sporting the world's largest diamond during a photoshoot...and little else.

Yet despite his predilection for obscene luxury, he also had the rare distinction of showing up to his office and working. The British division of Lykaois Shipping had soared under his guidance. He played hard, yes, but he worked just as hard.

Or at least had until a drunk driver had T-boned Griffith's Lamborghini, killing his father and leaving Griffith with severe injuries and a patchwork of scars. Some theorized a plastic surgeon would ensure that only the tiniest wounds would be visible. Others whispered that the reason Griffith had taken a leave of absence for an entire year had been because he was too ashamed to show his face in public.

The interview his ex-girlfriend Kacey Dupree had given less than two weeks ago certainly hadn't helped squash those rumors.

Whatever had happened, Griffith Lykaois had left behind his life of vice and hedonism for isolation.

She did feel sorry for him, had felt a kindred pain of loss when she'd read about the accident, seen the photos of twisted wreckage and bits of glass scattered across the road. But even if he wasn't engaging in decadent endeavors, he was still making selfish choices. Choices that had made her life hell, from the veiled threats from Mr. Nettleton about her future at the firm to the embarrassment of being escorted out of the Diamond Club.

She shook off her frustration and focused on the bittersweet, earthy scent of oak that filled the air, the occasional flash of warmth when a sunbeam fell across her face as she walked. She had been so driven for so long, so intent on working hard to get out of the town her parents had told her over and over was too small for what she was capable of, that she hadn't stopped to just breathe.

*Or think about what I wanted.*

Uncomfortable at the path her thoughts had taken, Rosalind shifted the strap of her bag to the other shoulder. It wasn't her parents' fault they had wanted the best for her. It wasn't their fault she had never gotten the courage to tell them she wanted something else. How could she, when they had looked at her with such pride? With hope that she would continue down the path they'd set for her.

*You'll be a senior lawyer at Nettleton & Thompson one day. I know it. You won't give up on that, will you?*

*I won't... I'll make you proud, Mom.*

Her parents had married young, scrimping and saving to buy a tiny house with a constantly leaking basement and three small bedrooms they'd crammed themselves and four kids into. Rosalind's older brother had been destined to follow in their father's footsteps as a lobster fisherman. Her two younger brothers had been adamant about going straight to work after high school, to make their own way.

It had fallen to Rosalind to achieve her parents' dream of having a child graduate college. A dream that had surpassed their wildest expectations when she'd been accepted into law school in Chicago, followed by the internship and then the job offer.

She'd never questioned herself before. Had simply accepted the praise they'd heaped on her, preened at the knowledge that her parents thought her so capable and merrily gone after each goal they encouraged her to reach for.

Her mother had lived long enough to see Rosalind try on her cap and gown the month before she graduated from law school, to learn about the job offer from Nettleton &

Thompson. Rosalind was on track to do exactly as her mother had wanted.

So, why didn't she feel excited by that?

All too soon, the lane curved and she emerged from the trees and turned to find herself in front of the gate. Constructed of wrought iron, and flanked by two stone pillars topped with statues, it certainly put the little white picket fence back home to shame. Her eyes traveled up, landing on the figures atop the stone pillars guarding either side of the drive—women garbed in dresses that reminded Rosalind of ancient Greek statues. Both statues had tumbling hair threaded through with what looked like stars. One woman held a rose clutched to her chest, while the other held a thorned flower up to the sky, as if offering it to the heavens.

A few hundred meters behind the gate lay the chateau, a sprawling manor house with rows of arched windows gleaming in the sun and topped off by a steep roof. Even at this distance, it exuded elegance. The kind of place her mother had described when she'd tell tales of princesses and princes, palaces and dungeons, enchantresses and beasts.

A brisk wind tore through the bars of the gate. She put her head down and shivered at the sudden coolness as heavy gray clouds scuttled across the sky and chased away the summer blue. An even bigger cluster of clouds loomed up behind the manor. Bonar had mentioned a storm moving in from the sea. But he had said it wouldn't hit until that evening.

She headed through the gate. She would get in, make her pitch and walk out with Lykaois's signature, and be back in Étretat before the storm really got going. Bonar had told her to call him if she needed a ride back to the village. Given how Lykaois had behaved so far, she doubted he would be so kind as to offer her a ride himself.

Rosalind took in more of the chateau as she got closer to it. Mr. Lykaois's New York penthouse sat on Billionaires' Row at the southern end of Central Park. It had been featured in a luxury real estate magazine, all glass walls and gleaming metal. The California beach house, fashioned in the shape of an L and colored gray, presided over a private beach and included a saltwater infinity pool that overlooked the Pacific. The Tokyo apartment overlooked Tokyo Tower and included access to a library, bar, spa and a private dining room serviced by international chefs.

So why had he chosen a centuries-old manor to hide out in? It was beautiful, yes. Expensive? Absolutely. Sweeping stone staircases trimmed in black railing framed either side of a three-tiered fountain. The steps curved up to a long terrace and massive double doors constructed of golden-brown wood with an arched window just above. The house had been maintained with not only great care but devotion to the original design. The final result was stunning.

But a very different feel from what Griffith Lykaois otherwise seemed to prefer. New, modern, flashy. Not historic and elegant.

Rosalind gripped the handle of her bag as she reached the stairs and started up. She needed to get her emotions under control. She'd had a strong reaction to him in the Diamond Club. But, as she'd told herself repeatedly in the days since, it had been understandable. Emotions had been running high. A lot was riding on her finally coming face-to-face with him and she'd read enough about the man, watched enough interviews from before his accident, to feel like she'd met him, knew him. Finally seeing him had pushed those emotions over the edge.

It made sense, too, that with her limited experience she would have a stronger response than the average woman. How often was anticipation better than the actual event?

Besides, she had other things to think about other than her hormones. Things like getting the contract signed and finally being promoted to midlevel associate attorney.

The thought of going back to London, of presenting the signed contract to Mr. Nettleton, should have buoyed her. Instead, it quickened her steps, as if she could outrun the restlessness that had been growing these past few months. Outrun the question that had been haunting her for months.

*Do I want to keep doing this?*

The strap of her bag pressed into her skin, the weight of her decision growing heavier with each step. She liked her work, liked hearing people's stories and what had become important to them over the course of their lives. Yet as time had gone on, the once dignified atmosphere of Nettleton & Thompson had started to feel more like a prison.

She had always considered herself a happy person. Even on days she'd slogged through thirteen hours of paperwork and client meetings, she'd been able to find the positives, like successfully navigating a will with a difficult client or watching the moon rise above the nearby Buckingham Palace.

But now...now she just felt exhausted.

The one positive in the struggle of reaching Mr. Lykaois was that she'd been able to put off confronting her dissatisfaction with her job just a while longer. To figure out if she wanted to work for the firm she had once thought she would retire from, or if she had the nerve to finally stop burying herself in work and make her own decision about what she wanted to do with her life. Live a little outside the walls of her office.

She shoved the questions away. Not the time to be having a personal crisis.

Now was the time to do her job.

She stopped in front of two massive wood doors.

*Here goes nothing.*

She raised the heavy knocker, a round loop of metal topped off with a sculpture of what looked like a rose, and let it fall.

No one answered.

Wind howled over the top of the manor, followed a moment later by scattered rain. Hunching her shoulders against the storm, she tried peering into one of the windows, but the curtains had been drawn tight. She went back to the door and knocked with her fist. One of the doors quivered, then slowly swung in.

She stood on the threshold, her hand tight around the handle of her briefcase. Technically no one had invited her in. But the door was open. And she'd come all this way after over a month of chasing the dratted man down.

Besides, it was starting to storm. Surely Mr. Lykaois would allow her to at least take shelter until the rain passed.

With a deep breath, she pushed the door wider and walked inside.

# CHAPTER FOUR

ROSALIND'S MOUTH DROPPED OPEN.

Mosaic tiles swirled into a stunning pattern of deep blues, vivid greens and elegant reds beneath her feet, contained by white stone edging the room. A matching stone staircase, wide enough to fit four people across, hugged the wall and spiraled up. The chandelier had been fashioned in black like the railing outside and hung from the ceiling a good fifteen feet above her head. Thankfully it was lit and kept the encroaching gloom from the storm at bay. The walls, painted a creamy ivory, caught the light and made the room glow. A long, thin table hugged one wall. The dark wood gleamed as if it had been freshly polished. Beautiful but bare, as if it were waiting for a bowl of fresh flowers or an antique vase.

The overall emptiness of the room struck her, made her sad. A stunning house with much to offer but left empty and alone.

She started to move about, too jittery to stay in one place. A painting caught her eye, one of the few adorning the walls of the hall. Well over four feet tall, it depicted white-capped waves surging onto a beach. The strokes that had captured the dark blue of an ocean at twilight had been fierce, the slashes depicting water churned up by the hint of dark clouds on the horizon. A cliff jutted out into the sea, proud and immovable against the water's wrath. The wildness spoke to her, sent a frisson of energy through her that rejuvenated her flagging spirits. It reminded her of the autumns of her childhood, with her nose pressed against the glass as she watched storms lash the Maine coast just steps away from her home. Fury and power, nature reminding man what it was capable of.

One lone figure had been painted on the small beach, a simple black shadow made strong with a tilted-up chin and shoulders thrown back, as though the person was confronting the ocean itself. It was tempting to reach out, to touch the character and encourage them to keep fighting.

A small smile flitted about her lips as she breathed in deeply. Whether she was projecting or not, the thought gave her a much-needed boost of determination to see her mission through.

A twinge settled between her shoulder blades. Awareness made her skin pebble as her breath caught in her chest. The same sensation she'd experienced in the Diamond Club right before she'd caught a glimpse of Griffith Lykaois lurking in the shadows. She hadn't seen his face, not clearly. That hadn't stopped the shock that had stolen her breath, the heat that had appeared out of nowhere and burned her skin.

The same heat now creeping over her, a fever that could only be assuaged by one decadent act she'd never experienced before.

She whirled around.

There was no one there.

"Miss Sutton."

The voice—deep, harsh, yet surprisingly melodic—rang out through the hall. It washed over her, slid under her skin and reverberated through her body like a deep roll of thunder.

Startled, she looked up. A man stood on the first landing of the grand staircase. A very tall man, his torso and face covered in shadow.

"Mr. Lykaois?"

"How did you gain entrance to this house?"

She tilted her head but couldn't make out any features. She had heard the rumors of his scars. One of the law clerks had even shown her the blurred photo published in last's week gossip magazine. But whether it had been out of focus intentionally or by accident, it had been hard to see much detail.

Curiosity nipped at her, but she quelled it. His scars, or lack thereof, were none of her business.

"The door was open."

One hand tightened on the railing. "So you trespassed."

Frustration reared its head. "Sir, I need to—"

"No." He stepped down onto the top stair, the shadows shifting up but still shielding his chest and head. "What you need to do, Miss Sutton, is leave before I call Nettleton & Thompson and tell them to fire you."

"For what?" she snapped.

Knowing he could do exactly as he'd threatened and that Mr. Nettleton would probably acquiesce in a heartbeat made her angry. She had worked hard, very hard, to get here. Regardless of her own doubts, that was the truth. She had tried to be nice, to be patient. But this man, who had the world at his fingertips, had thrown obstacles in her way at every juncture.

Determination lent strength to her voice. Irritation added an edge. "For doing my job? Going above and beyond by tracking you down across two countries?"

"If going against your client's wishes and stalking them is considered your job, then I'll take my business elsewhere."

Helplessness was an uncomfortable feeling. Helplessness coupled with anger was even more unpleasant. She could feel the words bubbling up in her throat, tried to stop them.

And then decided she didn't care anymore. If this was truly going to be the end of her career with Nettleton & Thompson, which at this point seemed inevitable no matter what she did, then she might as well go out in a blaze of glory and leave this spoiled playboy with a hint of the damage he'd caused.

"Until you sign this contract, my client is your father, or rather his estate." She reached into her bag and yanked out the thick sheaf of papers. "Since you haven't signed it, I don't care where you take your business. In fact," she added as she stepped forward and flung her head back, "I'd sincerely prefer you not do business with Nettleton & Thompson because you have been nothing but a pain in my butt."

Silence fell, save for the furious thudding of her heart in her chest.

Then, in a firm voice tinged with reluctant amusement, he said, "Really?"

"Really."

"And if you get fired?"

"If you don't sign, I'm fired. If you call Nettleton & Thompson, I'm fired." She threw up her hands in the air, barely keeping a grip on the contract. "So congratulations, you have me over a barrel."

"Over a barrel?"

She rolled her eyes. "Helpless. At your mercy."

"You don't sound helpless, Miss Sutton."

The heat trickled back in at the hint of admiration in his tone. Heat that only upped her irritation. How could she possibly be attracted to such an infuriating, self-absorbed man?

"I'm not helpless. I'm not a damsel in distress. I've continued forward through five canceled appointments, numerous hang-ups by your oh so efficient secretaries, and traveling over five hundred miles trying to track you down with my boss breathing down my neck and putting the future of my career in your hands. If I can survive that, I can survive anything."

Her chest rose and fell as she stared up at his shadowed face. She'd probably already signed her future away with her outburst. But God, it had felt good to finally vent her anger at his arrogance, at her career being reduced to her ability to get one simple signature.

She ran a hand through her curls and looked longingly at the partially open door before she turned back to him.

*One last time. Try to explain just one last time.*

"Do you not understand? If you don't sign, you'll lose everything—"

"I've already lost plenty, Miss Sutton." Cold suffused his words, all traces of amusement and admiration gone. He started walking down the stairs with slow, measured steps that made her chest tighten with dreaded anticipation. "My father. My girlfriend. My looks. My ability to walk in a crowd without scaring small children." The shadows crept up, revealed broad shoulders and a strong neck, the skin marred by one thick scar tinged pink. "What makes you think I give a damn about money anymore?"

And then he stepped into the light.

Rosalind pressed her lips together to stem her gasp. The scars on the right side of his face were made all the more distinct by the lack of damage to the left side. One scar started at his hairline and stabbed downward through his eyebrow. Miraculously, whatever had caused the wound had missed his eye, but just barely, judging by the way it slashed to his temple before traveling down over one carved cheekbone. Still another scar, a larger patch of red, was visible beneath his trimmed beard, snaking from mouth to jaw and then farther down.

Jarring, yes. But the way the tabloid had played it up, including a lurid description from his former girlfriend, had made him sound like a beast or Frankenstein's monster.

To her, he looked like a man who had suffered, yet survived, a horrific car accident.

"If you don't want the money, then I need your signature on a different document relinquishing any claims on the inheritance."

Surprise flitted across his face. Had he expected her to run away screaming?

"Did you not hear me, Miss Sutton?" He raised his chin even as he managed to look down his still-aristocratic nose at her. "I'm not signing it. Any of it."

*Fine.* If the man wanted to refuse billions of dollars, money that people like her parents and her neighbors back in Maine could have used to do so much with, then that was his choice. That he would prefer to throw it away rather than put it to good use angered her further and added acid to her next words.

"Then use it for something else. Drawing. Writing poetry. Perhaps making paper airplanes. My nephews get a kick out of that sort of thing."

"Do I look like the kind of man who writes poetry?" he growled.

"No."

She took a risk as she moved to the bottom of the staircase and looked up at him. He stood a few stairs above her. The light from the chandelier highlighted the left side of his face from the unblemished warm ivory of his skin to the sharp line of his jaw. Dark golden hair, thick and slightly tousled, fell over his broad forehead.

Her anger bled away. It almost seemed crueler to leave him with half of his former face. A constant reminder of who he had been.

Their gazes collided. Her heart stuttered in her chest. The heat returned, spread throughout her body and made her limbs heavy, drugged her with desire.

She blinked and stepped back, trying to get her bearings, to summon something akin to professionalism after her eruption. The scar by Griffith's mouth twisted as his lips curled back into a sneer.

"Then what kind of man do I look like, Miss Sutton?" He came down until he was just one step above her, only inches between them. "A spoiled bastard who got what was coming to him? Or maybe something simpler? A monster, perhaps?"

The last words, raw and guttural, stopped her anger in its tracks. Her gaze moved over him, registered the taut cords of muscle in his neck, the tension in his jaw twisting his scars. And behind the patrician gleam of disdain in his eyes…pain. Deep, horrible pain.

The remnants of her anger dissipated, slipped away, left her wanting to reach out and offer something, anything, to lessen the burden of such profound agony.

"No. You look like someone who's hurting."

His face twisted into an expression of disgust that made her feel small and insignificant. He stared at her, chest rising and falling, a pulse pounding in his throat. She could almost feel his heartbeat, feel the anguish that kept him in an iron grip.

Her eyes traveled from his throat up to the scarred, handsome face, her breath catching as his glittering gaze ensnared her.

"I said no. I'm not signing."

For a moment she just stared at him. Dimly she heard a howl of wind, the deeper rumble of thunder warning that the storm was getting closer.

Finally, the cold words registered and snapped her out of her reverie. Her fury returned, eclipsing her surroundings as she let go of any hope of keeping her job.

"I would be curious to see how a man who's had everything handed to him on a diamond-encrusted platter would handle throwing out a mere mortal like myself. But no matter," she continued as his lips parted on a retort. "I've literally traipsed hundreds of miles, stood out in the pouring rain and argued with your employees the world over to just get one signature. And I'm done."

She held up the contract. Common sense whispered for her to stop, to hold back, but no. She was done playing nice with such a selfish man.

She let go, savored the thump when the file hit the table as much as she enjoyed the widening of his eyes, the thinning of his mouth.

"Have a good day, Mr. Lykaois."

She shot him a megawatt smile, inclined her head to him and then walked out of the chateau.

# CHAPTER FIVE

GRIFFITH STARED AT the open door. He couldn't recall the last time someone had walked away from him. That she had done so with an attitude, acting as if *he'd* wronged *her* when she'd been the one to stalk him across the Channel and trespass on his land, had him stride across the hall to shut the door on Miss Rosalind Sutton once and for all.

He reached the door, then glanced back at the contract on the table. A seemingly innocuous stack of papers that he wanted nothing to do with. Signing them would bring an end to this mess. Stop Miss Sutton's relentless campaign.

Although if her parting words were any indication, she had no intention of seeing him ever again. Which should make him relieved.

But it didn't. Instead, the emptiness of the house pressed in on him, as did the roar of the storm growing outside. The thought of never seeing Rosalind again, a woman who had made such an incredible impact in a matter of minutes, sent an unexpected pang through the hollowness of his chest.

*Damn it.*

Lightning pierced the sky, followed seconds later by thunder that rattled the windows. Griffith stopped in the doorway. In the few minutes since he had come downstairs to confront Rosalind, the encroaching storm had darkened the summery landscape. Wind howled around the corner of the chateau and tore at the tops of nearby trees.

He might be a selfish bastard. But he couldn't send the lawyer away in this, could he. It was a long way back to the village and an image of her battling the wind and the rain, fighting to stay upright, came to mind. Going after her was the right thing to do, he didn't need to like it.

Griffith started down the steps, his eyes sweeping over the freshly mowed lawn, the neatly trimmed hedges bordering the front yard, the dry yet still elegant fountain, for any signs of a caramel-colored trench coat or mahogany brown curls.

Nothing. Aside from the whimsical fairy that perched on top of the fountain, he was alone.

Had she double backed and found another way into the house? Or discovered the covered patio on the north side of the house?

Movement caught his eye. His lips parted in surprise as he saw a distant figure moving toward the avenue of trees.

"Miss Sutton!" he bellowed. "Rosalind!"

The wind snatched away his words as Rosalind disappeared into the trees. Cursing, he hurried down the steps. As soon as his feet hit the drive, he ran.

He'd been a runner before the accident, had hopped back on the treadmill as soon as the doctor had cleared him. But the machine, useful as it was for letting him run while avoiding prying eyes or paparazzi, was nothing compared to the freedom of being outside, of feeling the cool whip of the wind across his face as blood pumped hot in his veins.

*Alive.*

He'd taken so much for granted. Lost so much.

*Not this. Not yet.*

He should let her go. Let her walk away.

*Not yet.*

Cold raindrops fell on the back of his neck. Light, but the pace picked up as he entered the avenue. Up ahead, Rosalind continued moving at a brisk pace toward the bridge.

"Miss Sutton!"

She turned, a frown appearing between her brows. She stopped and faced him, the hem of her trench coat flapping about her knees. For one wild moment, he saw her as something more, something magical and mysterious. With the wind grabbing her curls and whipping them about her beautiful face, the stubborn tilt to her pointed chin, the sparkle of life in her dark green eyes, she reminded him of an enchantress or a mischievous fairy.

"Making sure I actually leave?"

"Come back until the storm's over."

She stared at him, her lips slightly parting.

"Excuse me?"

He could barely hear her over the wind, the thunder that clashed far too close for comfort.

"It's too dangerous for you to walk. The nearest petrol station is over three kilometers away."

"You told me to go. I wouldn't want to stay where I wasn't welcome."

"That was before I realized how bad the storm was."

She shook her head even as she squinted against the shrieking wind whipping down the avenue. "I have no interest in being around you, Mr. Lykaois. I can make it to the road, call my ride and be gone before the storm gets worse."

"The storm is coming too fast. Don't be foolish."

Her eyes turned molten with anger. Before she could utter a retort, lightning flashed above their heads, spearing down through the canopy and striking the trunk of one of the trees. Thunder followed, deep and fierce. It nearly covered the sharp crack as bark splintered and the tree shifted.

He lunged, wrapped his arms around Rosalind's waist and tackled her to the ground as the towering oak shuddered and fell. They landed on the crushed shells of the drive and rolled. He kept her body pinned to his, planted his feet and stopped so that he lay on top of her.

The ground shook beneath them. He raised his head. The oak lay just a few feet away.

He turned his attention back to Rosalind. She lay beneath him, face white, eyes wide as she stared at the tree.

"Are you all right?"

Slowly, she nodded. She looked at him, then down at their bodies pressed together. A blush stole over her cheeks. The sight summoned the desire that had invaded earlier as she'd stood in the hall, beautiful in her kindness, frightening in her perceptiveness, stunning in her defiance.

He quickly shifted, rolling off her before she felt the evidence of his arousal. Standing, he held out his hand and pulled her to her feet.

His eyes followed hers to the fallen tree. Before they'd even set eyes on the house, his mother had fallen in love with the towering oaks. His father had joked they didn't even need the house, just the trees.

Centuries. The tree had stood for centuries, withstood

war and changing seasons, birth and death in the manor just beyond.

Now it lay on the ground, chunks of bark scattered across the seashells like dark wounds.

A vise clamped around his heart, squeezed. His gaze moved over the leaves still clinging to the branches, then down to the jagged edges of where the tree had split from the trunk, portions of it blackened by the lightning's fury.

Foolish to get sentimental over a damned tree.

He turned his back on it, focused his attention on the woman who had drawn him out into the storm.

"Miss Sutton—"

The clouds unleashed their fury, the rain turning from a spatter to a downpour. It was impossible to see more than a few feet ahead. He grabbed her hand and yanked her forward. When she resisted, tried to pull away, he tightened his grip and tugged her close until her body pressed against his.

"We need to get back to the chateau." His lips nearly brushed her ear.

"I'm not five," she retorted. "I can make my own—"

"And get separated in this rain? Tumble into a ravine? Catch pneumonia?"

"Are those possibilities or personal fantasies?"

"My fantasy is to be warm, dry and not worrying about whether you're wandering my property or lying under a tree."

He pulled her forward again. She followed, keeping pace with his long strides as he kept his eyes on the seashells. He followed the path, catching glimpses here and there of familiar shapes beyond the rain.

Then, at last, light pierced the darkness. The lanterns on the front wall of the house glowed gold in the deluge. They stumbled up the stairs and into the grand hall. Griffith slammed the door behind them.

And immediately realized he was trapped in a hell of his own making.

Rosalind stood in the center of the hall, water dripping from her trench coat onto the tiled floor. A leaf clung to one wet curl. Mud coated her knees and streaked her calves. She stared at him with intense dislike, her lips pursed as if she was trying to hold back one of her pithy insults.

And he had never wanted a woman more than he did in that moment. A woman who had ensnared him with just the sound of her voice and her fierce tenacity in the face of adversity. Adversity he had created to keep her and everything she represented at arm's length.

Instead of faltering, she'd hit back stronger and harder. Then, when he'd resorted to petty threats, she'd stood up to him and told him exactly where to stick it.

He didn't want to like her. Didn't want to admire her. Didn't want to imagine stripping off that coat, leading her upstairs and into his palatial shower, leaving a trail of wet clothes as he pulled her beneath a steaming hot spray and—

*Stop!*

Indulging in those kinds of thoughts would only make this more difficult.

Although, he realized as he glanced around the hall, the situation was about as difficult as it could be. From what he'd been able to see, the tree had landed on the bridge. He would go down after the storm had passed to confirm his suspicions. But if that were true, they were stranded at the chateau until next week when the housekeeper, Beatrice, and her husband journeyed up from their village to bring food and clean.

A hard knot formed at the base of his spine as a headache began to pound away at his temples. When he'd contacted Beatrice and told her he was coming for an extended stay, she'd reminded him the chateau didn't have internet and had very unreliable cell phone reception. He'd told her those conditions would work perfectly for the isolation he sought.

Except now it had left him alone with a woman as tempting as she was infuriating...

"I'll show you to a room so you can change."

"If you just tell me—"

"No!" The thought of a stranger wandering through the house—his mother's house—filled him with anger.

Rosalind watched him from her place by the door. She didn't tremble, didn't look away. The longer she watched him, *stared* at him, the angrier he became. Angry at her being in his house, the one place that was supposed to be safe. Angry at himself for displaying such raw emotion. Angry at the world for constantly taking, punishing, driving him closer and closer to the edge.

"Follow me," he growled.

He knew he was overreacting, despised himself as much as he despised her seemingly calm demeanor. She'd walked into a fierce storm, nearly been crushed by a tree and now followed a scarred, hollowed husk of a man up a staircase into a strange house. A man who had threatened to have her fired and, by her account, made her life miserable. Not once had she cried or complained. Up until twenty minutes ago, her name had been synonymous with irritation. The uptight, overzealous lawyer with a ridiculous umbrella who couldn't leave well enough alone.

But now…now he saw more of what he'd glimpsed that day in the Diamond Club. Confidence, strength, resilience.

*No.* He had survived the past year without sex, without extravagance, without anything from his old life. Too little, too late, but at least he was doing something to honor Belen. To be the man he should have been instead of the indulgent bastard who had kept his father at arm's length.

His lust for Rosalind threatened his self-imposed punishment. A whim that he would not allow himself to satisfy.

He stalked down the hallway and stopped in front of a white door trimmed in gold filigree.

"Here." He twisted the knob and opened the door. "Power should stay on with the generator—"

"Oh!"

Her breathless exclamation cut him off midsentence. She moved past him into the room, spun around in a circle with wide eyes and parted lips. Her wet hair framed her face, delicate in its shape but countered by the narrow, strong point of her chin. Rain dripped from the hem of her trench coat onto the plush wool and silk Persian carpet. She looked nothing like the sophisticated, discerning women he had dated over the years.

He shouldn't want her. Couldn't want her. Didn't deserve to want her. He could hardly stand to look at himself in the mirror, share his bed with a woman. Indulging his own whims, his own desire, was out of the question.

Rosalind shot him a huge smile, one that made her eyes crinkle at the corners and a tiny dimple appear on one side of her mouth.

"This room is incredible." Her eyes softened. "Thank you, Mr. Lykaois. For saving—"

"Don't."

The smile faded from her face. A part of him mourned the loss, wanted to do something to bring back the radiance.

But that would only prolong the torture.

"You're staying here so you don't get killed on my property and someone sues."

The words tasted sharp, bitter. The brief flicker of surprise and pity in her eyes drove it home.

"Of course." She turned her back to him then, dismissing him. "I'll be gone as soon as the storm clears."

She didn't even look at him as she turned and moved to the window, pulled aside the filmy curtain to gaze out into the wall of rain.

Griffith strode out, managing to refrain from slamming the door behind him as he headed for the stairs. Miss Sutton had already stirred up his emotions, piqued his curiosity. She hadn't flinched at the sight of his face, true. But what would she do if she saw the worst of the wounds that cut over his ribs, snaked along his thigh and down his leg?

It didn't matter. She would never see them. He wouldn't allow himself to surrender to the inferno raging through him. Not with the woman who wanted him to acknowledge that his father was gone, her actions rubbing salt in the wound of his culpability.

*If I would have been paying attention...if I wouldn't have been angry...*

It didn't change anything. Never would. His father wasn't coming back.

He entered the library and set about making a fire. The rough scrape of the wood on his palms, the scent of smoke, grounded him, gave him something to focus on beside thoughts of Miss Sutton moving about on the floor above.

He hurled the last log onto the fire. Sparks shot up, glittering red and orange and crackling up into the air before falling back down. Some littered the edge of the hearth, pulsing with a hypnotic glow.

Rosalind was the kind of woman he had always stayed away from. The kind of woman who wanted compassion, affection, love. Things he was incapable of giving. Her enthrallment with her room, her gratitude and, most telling of all, her perception of his pain before she'd walked out into the storm, told him all he needed to know. Fierce but kind. Determined but empathetic.

She deserved someone who could fulfill her needs, not just physical but emotional. When he'd withdrawn into himself following his mother's death, latched on to the solidity of his vices, the immediate distraction and pleasure they brought, he knew he'd been turning his back on the traditional things: a wedding, marriage, children. Now, even if he wanted to change that, he'd lived a life of isolation for so long he couldn't feel much of anything except the rawness of grief and intensity of self-loathing.

He stopped in front of the window, stared out at the wind-tossed sea. Then saw his reflection in the glass. His hand came up, touched the ugly ridges of the largest scar that snaked down his face. Scars that had disgusted Kacey, caused more than one person in his life to look away, unable to meet his eyes without staring.

Rosalind hadn't. She'd faced him without flinching. He hadn't missed the answering flicker of desire in her own eyes. What would she do if she knew the extent of his own lust? The almost animalistic need to claim her body, which had seethed beneath the surface ever since he'd seen her in London?

Miss Sutton had nothing to fear from his visible scars. It was the cold, dark bastard who lurked inside him who should frighten her most of all.

# CHAPTER SIX

ROSALIND AWOKE TO a faint glow behind the curtains. She lay still beneath the comforter, luxuriating in the feel of actual silk against her skin.

When she'd walked into the room the night before, it had been like walking into a fairy tale. Hardwood floors with streaks of gray and tan had gleamed beneath the light of an actual chandelier hanging from the tall ceiling. Antique furniture in various shades of blue and trimmed in toffee-colored wood, from the navy chairs situated in front of a white stone fireplace to a periwinkle blue fainting couch arranged in front of the massive windows, had been polished to perfection. Paintings adorned the walls, all of them featuring various seascapes or the surrounding cliffs.

And the bed…the glorious bed had sat on a raised dais with actual curtains gathered with gold ropes at the corners. The number of pillows would have made her father and brothers roll their eyes.

But it had been perfect. Even with the ocean obscured by the rain and the gloominess of the man who had escorted her upstairs, it had eased the iron grip that tension had kept on her chest since she'd dropped the file on the table and left the chateau.

It had also been a much-needed balm for the chaos that had scraped her heart raw in just one hour. She'd lost control and insulted the highest profile client she'd ever worked for. Then, when she'd been so close to freedom, she'd almost been crushed by an ancient oak.

And rescued by the very man she'd offended moments before.

She pulled a pillow over her face and groaned into it. Yes, it had been terrifying to realize how close she'd come to getting hurt or even killed during the storm. But she'd lived through her fair share of nor'easters and even the occasional hurricane growing up on Maine's rugged coast. She'd learned resilience at a young age.

What unsettled her more was her reaction to Griffith and his unexpected bravery. The man had gone from selfish bastard to selfless hero with one act. It had confused her, made some of the respect and curiosity she'd experienced when she'd first researched him resurface.

His anger, too, had intrigued her. Not that she was going to put up with being his emotional punching bag for whatever issues he was dealing with. But his reaction to her being in the chateau, to her appreciation for the room, had seemed rooted in something other than simple selfishness. As she'd told him before she had—yes, foolishly—walked out into the storm, he seemed like he was in pain. Not just grief, but something more, something deeper.

Frustrated with herself for ruminating on him, she sat up and tossed a pillow across the room. What was the point in thinking about him? Wasting time and energy theorizing about his hang-ups when he had made it clear he wanted her gone as soon as she was able to? Honestly, she thought as she threw back the covers, it was a good thing he'd left her alone last night. She'd been vulnerable, susceptible to her feelings of gratitude and attraction. Yes, the man was ridiculously handsome. But she had held out this long on having sex. Had rebuffed advances from men far kinder as she waited for the right one, the one she felt both an emotional and physical connection to. When she finally took a lover, it would be someone she could potentially see a future with.

No matter how intriguing or exciting Griffith Lykaois was, he was the exact opposite definition of a long-term boyfriend. He would tempt a woman to indulge, enjoy, lose herself in pleasure.

And then he'd be gone just as quickly as he'd arrived.

What she needed to do now was get up, gather her things and get out of here. Make a plan for how she would drop the news to Mr. Nettleton about the unsigned contract. Make a contingency plan in case he decided to fire her or in case Griffith had already called to demand the same thing.

She stopped her runaway thoughts. Breathed in deep. *You had a bath in an actual claw-foot tub last night. Focus on the positives.*

Her stomach rumbled. She had eaten a late lunch in Étretat before she'd set out for the Chateau du Belle-rose. The chaos of the afternoon, including dealing with Griffith Lykaois and nearly getting squished by a centuries-old oak, had driven any thoughts of hunger from her head. After she'd gotten out of the tub, exhaustion had enticed her into bed.

She slipped out from under the sheets and the pleasant weight of the down comforter. Cool air kissed her bare skin. It had been odd sleeping nude, but her clothes had been soaked, from her favorite coat down to her underwear. She pulled a light, airy blanket off the corner of the bed and wrapped it around her body as she moved to the windows. She drew back the curtains.

And caught her breath.

Behind the house lay an incredible garden, one full of winding paths made of what looked like the same crushed seashells as the drive and encircled by a towering ivy hedge. There were occasional trees, including a willow with long strands of leaves that flirted with the surface of a pond. Benches had been added, too, and an occasional statue.

But the pièce de résistance was the roses. Hundreds and hundreds of roses in varying shades of red, pink and white. Crimson blooms climbed over a stone archway. Softer colored flowers that reminded her of ballet slippers spilled from a stone urn. Ivory roses adorned row after row of bushes.

Grief slid in, quiet at first. But it grew, slow and steady, until her body was heavy and her joy disappeared.

She moved to the windows and leaned her head against the cool glass. It had been two years since she'd gotten the first phone call from her father. Her mother had come down with a mild but persistent fever just a month after recovering from what had seemed to be a mild bout of pneumonia. She'd video-called home, seen Mom propped up in bed and rolling her eyes as Dad had fussed over her. Her mom had asked her about her classes, if she was dating anyone, the mother-daughter railroad trip they had planned for the summer that would take them from Italy to Monaco.

It had all seemed so ordinary. Just a simple fever.

Then the second phone call had come at two in the morning. The tension in her father's voice, the hint of panic underlying his thick Maine accent, had set her nerves on edge before he'd even told her that her mother's fever had spiked and she was in the hospital. It was the first time her mother had been to a hospital in over two decades, the last time for the birth of Rosalind's youngest brother.

Rosalind had hung up and started packing as she purchased a ticket home. She'd been walking into the airport when her phone had rung again.

"Rose…"

Goose bumps had covered Rosalind's arms as her mother's raspy voice descended into a coughing fit.

"Mom?"

"Darling… I'm so proud of you."

"I know, Mom."

"Never stop living your life to the fullest. Reaching for…reaching for those goals."

Another hacking cough came over the line, sending cold fingers of fear down Rosalind's spine.

"You'll be a senior lawyer at Nettleton & Thompson one day. I know it. You won't give up on that, will you?"

"I won't." Her fingers tightened around the phone as her heart hammered in her chest. "I'll make you proud, Mom. And when we go to Italy this summer we'll—"

"Italy…" Her mother's voice turned dreamy, as if coming from some faraway place. "Such a fun trip."

"Mom…"

"Yes, darling?"

She stood in the middle of Chicago's O'Hare Airport, passengers streaming by, tears pouring down her face as she clung to her phone, like if she held tight enough she could keep her mother tethered to this earth through sheer will.

"I love you, Mom."

"I love you, my baby girl. My pretty rose."

Rosalind closed her eyes against the hot sting of tears. Time had softened the sharpest edges of her grief. Yet there were times like now, moments she knew her mother would have embraced with a delighted smile and a hearty laugh, that brought it rushing back as if it were yesterday.

She'd known when her father had taken the phone from her mother, had told her that things weren't going well, that she wasn't going to make it. That hadn't stopped her from boarding the flight and paying the extra charge for Wi-Fi to stay in touch with her brothers as she'd flown north.

The plane had been just south of the Great Lakes when she'd gotten the message. Her mother, her biggest champion and her best friend, had passed. She'd spent the rest of the flight with her face turned to the window, tears streaming silently down her cheeks.

She opened her eyes and stared out at the sea. The weeks she'd spent at home had passed in a gray haze, with many hours spent on the dock that jutted out into the bay, sometimes crying, other times just staring at the horizon. Always awash in grief, an aching loss that haunted her every waking moment.

She'd always been able to see the good in everything, to focus on the positive, just like her mother. But this…it had shaken her foundation, introduced true sorrow into her life. Moving to London, to her internship at Nettleton & Thompson, had been the lifeline she'd desperately needed to pull her out of her heartache. She'd thrown herself into her work. Knowing that she had made her parents proud, that she had achieved everything her mother had dreamed for her, had kept her going for the past two years.

And it had sustained her. At least to start with. It hadn't stopped discontent from starting to creep in, to fester, especially in the last month or so. A feeling that in her quest to be a responsible, mature individual, to do everything her parents had expected of her, she'd missed out on something crucial.

She was liked well enough at work, occasionally shared lunch with her coworkers. But she didn't go out with them for dinner, to clubs or on weekend trips to the Continent. She rarely dated. When she did, it was someone she had met through work. Conversations inevitably turned to the legal field and the dates ended up feeling more like a job interview than something romantic.

Even the one thing she did make time for, reading, had become a chore instead of a source of relaxation as she'd prepared herself for a potential promotion. Instead of romances and cozy mysteries, she'd read legal briefs, case studies and samples of wills until she could recite them in her sleep.

She was good at finding the happy things in life. But when was the last time she had enjoyed a long lunch? Said yes to a coworker's invitation to go out or traveled outside the comforts of London?

*A year. Maybe more.*

Past the garden lay a meadow of tall grasses swaying in the breeze. Then a cliff, and beyond that the ocean, the same deep and mesmerizing blue as the pillows on her bed, the throw tossed over one of the chairs by the fireplace.

Her brows drew together. Someone had gone to a great deal of trouble to maintain this house, keep it in working order. Yet from what she could tell, Griffith Lykaois was the only person in residence. He hadn't been here in the past month. Did he pay to have someone keep it like this?

If so, why? Did he come here often? Why this place and not one of his other properties?

She shook her head. It didn't matter. Griffith Lykaois's intentions and preferences were his own. The only choice she cared about was whether or not he signed for his inheritance.

A thought came as she turned away from the window and the spectacular view, one that filled her with resolve and cautious hope. As much as she could have done without the almost getting flattened by a tree, she could see the storm had been a blessing. It had given her a second chance to catch her breath, refocus her attention and secure his signature before she left.

Concentrating on business had the added benefit of shifting her attention away from the memory of Griffith's brooding stare and the decadent desire he could inspire with a single glance.

She padded into the bathroom. Another work of art, she thought with a small smile, and larger than her childhood living room. The claw-foot tub she'd soaked in last night had been installed before a bay of windows, which, by the light of day, she could now see also overlooked the rose garden and the sea. A shower made of black tile and a wall of glass with not one but two waterfall showerheads in the ceiling took up most of the back wall. Marble counters and gleaming silver fixtures shone under the glow of elegant wall sconces.

A distant knock pulled her out of her reverie. She walked out into the bedroom just as the door swung open.

"Wait!"

"Miss Sutton…"

Griffith's voice trailed off as his eyes landed on her blanket-clad figure.

Shock froze her in place. His gaze moved from her face down to the thin material she clutched to her breasts.

The atmosphere shifted, heated as his eyes sharpened, traveled down over her legs and bare feet before moving back up to her face. Her nipples hardened into tight points and pressed against the fabric. Mortification and desire clashed, melded into a heat that spread throughout her body.

Their gazes met, locked. In the bright light of day, his scars were more vivid. Most were paler in color, but the one that cut through a thick brow and around his eye was still red.

The wounds didn't detract from his sheer handsomeness. They added complexity, depth to the chiseled features. The cleft in his chin interrupted the nearly perfect line of a strong jaw covered by a well-trimmed beard.

And his eyes…right now they glimmered, a dark blue that somehow burned as he watched her.

A voice whispered in her ear, dared her to do something outrageous like let the blanket fall. To place the ball in his court and see what happened next. She'd been waiting her whole life for the right man, the perfect man, to share her body with. Each man she'd gone to dinner with, kissed, had fallen short somehow. Some had simply not been a good fit. Others had been cordial, kind, interesting.

But none had done this. Set her body aflame with a single look.

"I knocked."

"I didn't hear you."

God, was that her voice? Breathless, husky?

"The tree fell onto the bridge."

She blinked and just like that, the fire was gone from

his eyes. The cold, controlled man from the night was back, his voice authoritative and sterile.

"What?"

"The tree," he repeated, as if she was a child not paying attention. "It fell onto the bridge."

Unease fluttered in her stomach.

"So…what does that mean?"

"It means until someone can come up here and remove the tree and test the bridge, make sure it's safe, you're to remain here."

She stifled her alarm, took in a deep breath.

"Okay. I understand. When will someone be by?"

"Probably a week."

Her mouth dropped open.

"A week?"

"Yes."

"But…why so long?"

"Because that will be the first time Madame Beatrice and her husband will be back to restock the kitchen and any missing supplies."

"Why don't we just call someone?"

"No reception." He arched a brow. The scar added a dangerous, almost thrilling edge to the gesture. "Surely you noticed last night?"

"When I was walking up, yes, but I assumed you'd have reception here."

"No. Eventually I'll have something installed out here for phone and internet."

Unease morphed into dread.

"I can't just stay here."

"Unless you plan on climbing down into a one-hundred-foot gorge before scaling the other side, or swimming around the cliffs to the nearest beach, you're not going anywhere."

"What if there's an emergency?"

He shrugged. "It was supposed to be just me."

The part that went unsaid, that he appeared to care less whether or not something happened to him, stirred her sympathy. They'd both lost a parent, but he was now alone in the world. No brothers to call and tease him, no father to send small gifts from back home.

"I'm sorry."

He blinked, as if surprised by her apology.

"Too late now."

Her sympathy evaporated.

"Are you always this charming?"

"Always."

Her eyes narrowed. Could that have been a hint of humor in his voice?

*It doesn't matter.*

She had seven more days to get the contract signed and back to London. If the housekeeper and her husband made it up in six days, that left her one day. One day for the tree to be removed, the bridge deemed safe and for her to get back home.

Her mind scrambled, tried to find a solution that wasn't foolish or unsafe but didn't cut it so close to her deadline.

And came up with zilch.

"Okay." She squared her shoulders. She'd faced down bickering relatives and bloodthirsty rivals in the legal world. She could handle one week at a remote chateau with a less than friendly host. "What do we do?"

He shrugged. "I don't care what you do. You may use the common spaces and the grounds. Help yourself to what's in the kitchen. But," he said, his voice dropping into something dark and almost menacing, "stay off the third floor. My office and private quarters."

"I'll have no trouble with that," she grumbled under her breath.

"And don't expect me to entertain you."

"I have no desire to be entertained by you," she shot back with a sweet smile. "The only thing I desire is your signature on one contract or the other so that after this unfortunate week is over, we can never see each other again."

A laugh escaped him, dry and rough, as if he hadn't used his voice for such a purpose in a very long time.

"You're trying to discuss business while you're wearing nothing but a blanket?"

She narrowed her eyes at him. "It certainly beats my only alternative at the moment."

No sooner had the words left her mouth than his eyes slid down again to her breasts. The tension returned, so hot and heavy it was a wonder she didn't start sweating. His hands clenched, unclenched by his sides. It wasn't the only sign that he was affected by what she'd just said. Her own gaze wandered over the dark gray sweater that clung to his broad chest, the hint of hair curling at the base of his throat, then farther down still to the noticeable bulge beneath his black pants.

She swallowed hard. She wasn't a stranger to what happened when men grew aroused. The last time she'd gone out and her date had pulled her close for a long kiss goodnight, she'd felt how much he'd wanted her pressed against her lower belly. The weight of his desire had sparked nothing but a mild curiosity. She certainly hadn't been curious enough to take things further.

Now, though, just the sight of Griffith's hard length

straining against his pants had her own thighs growing damp with arousal.

"Don't you have something else to wear?" he snapped.

She lifted her chin up in the air. He was the one who had invaded her privacy.

"Once my dress is dry, yes."

He turned and walked out, slamming the door behind him. She released a pent-up breath.

*What was that?*

A shudder moved through her body, delicious and slightly wild. Never had she been tempted to do something as audacious as seduce a man. Let him see all of her. Let him see how quickly and easily she had been turned on by his presence. That had been part of the problem— really *the* problem—with the men she'd dated. None of them had made her feel the way she wanted to feel with her first lover. They checked the boxes of kind, attentive, thoughtful. But the physical attraction, the desire, had never appeared.

Her roommate in college had told her on numerous occasions her expectations were too high. Her mother had told her to trust herself. That when she found the right man, she would know.

Not someone like *him*. Brooding, solitary and downright rude. Although, she thought with a twist of her lips, he had at least done her the favor of showing her what was possible.

A carnal image appeared in her mind, of Griffith yanking the blanket from her hands, scooping her up in his arms and lowering her to the bed, before standing back and peeling his sweater away from chiseled abs—

Three loud knocks sounded on her door. He was back.

She waited for Griffith to storm back in, to renew their argument, but he didn't. Silence reigned.

Finally, she walked across the room and cracked the door. A trunk—an actual steamer trunk—sat in front of the door. It had been painted an olive green and trimmed in black leather with gold accents. But there was no sign of Griffith.

Keeping one hand firmly on the blanket, she grabbed hold of one black leather handle and pulled the trunk inside, casting one more glance up and down the hall before closing the door and locking it. She undid the latch and pushed the lid up.

A rainbow of material greeted her. She reached down, ran a finger over red silk, periwinkle linen and daisy-yellow cotton. One by one she pulled out dresses, skirts, shirts and a pair of pants, until nearly twenty garments lay across the bed. All of them still had tags attached, all sporting the same floral design and the name of a designer she knew only by reputation. The kind of designer with a storefront on Bond Street in London's high-end Mayfair district.

Did Griffith keep clothes around for potential visiting lovers? She should be thankful he had anything for her to wear at all, but the thought made her surprisingly irritated. Pushing it aside, she settled on a forest green dress with matching buttons running from the sweetheart neckline over the cinched waist and down to the hem of the full skirt. Simple yet luxurious as she dropped the blanket and pulled the dress on, the linen caressing her skin.

She moved to the full-length mirror by the fireplace. Spun in a circle and grinned as the skirt flared out.

It was not how she had planned on spending her time in France. But with a trunk full of designer clothes she'd never get to wear again, a stunning bedroom overlooking the sea and nearly a week to convince Mr. Griffith Lykaois to sign, things were certainly looking up.

With that encouraging thought in mind, she turned and picked the blanket up off the floor. The feel of the fabric in her hands made her remember Griffith's heated gaze fixed on her breasts, his jaw tight and his fingers curled into fists at his sides, as if he could barely hold himself back.

Her hands tightened on the blanket before she balled it up and threw it into a corner. She could have a good week, could make it into something positive, if she kept her erotic imagination under control.

A walk, she decided. She'd go for a walk first.

And hope the cool sea air would knock some sense into her, starting with the fact that she had a job to do and Griffith Lykaois was the last man on earth she should be fantasizing about.

# CHAPTER SEVEN

GRIFFITH'S FINGERS TIGHTENED around his pen as the sound of a door closing drifted in through the open window. Unless a ghost had taken up residence, it could only be one person.

He would prefer the ghost. Perhaps it would haunt him less than Miss Rosalind Sutton.

He hadn't seen her in two days. Not since the morning she'd walked out of the en suite bathroom clad in nothing but that gauzy blue blanket that had clung to the curves of her breasts and wrecked his control.

Never had he wanted a woman as badly as he'd wanted her in that moment. Sunlight had pierced the thin material, highlighted the nip to her waist, the flare of her hips, her long legs. Her curls had had a mind of their own, spreading around her head like an auburn-colored halo.

And those eyes…large, framed by dark lashes, innocent.

The answering heat that had flickered in the green depths had catapulted his lust into something so fierce and reckless he'd had no choice but to leave. His self-control was resting on a knife's edge. Retreating was the only option. It was what he was good at. Keeping himself out of emotion's way.

Surprisingly, she had left him alone. It was for the best. At least that was what Griffith told himself as he tried to focus on anything but the woman whose mere presence tormented him.

Fortunately, he had plenty to do, even without the modern wonders of technology. He had brought printouts of finances, shipping routes and summaries from each of the members of the executive boards, which he'd requested a month ago. Summaries that included what they had achieved during his sabbatical, what they wanted to change and, most importantly, what they wanted to see in the future. His father had done the company proud, had celebrated success even as he'd kept a constant eye on opportunities to grow. A continuation of the legacy Griffith's grandfather had started when he'd turned a few shipping boats into an empire. A legacy Griffith was determined to follow.

*You don't deserve to lead. You're not even half the man they were.*

He smothered the intrusive thoughts. He hadn't been deserving before. But he would be. He would never make the same selfish mistakes ever again.

Having work to focus on would also help him maintain control.

With that resolution in mind, he'd sat down at the oversize walnut desk, three levels of bookcases soaring up to the ceiling in front of him and the large windows overlooking the rose garden at his back. An ideal environment to jot down notes and make the most of his sudden desire to be productive.

Except every time he sat down to work, thoughts interfered. Thoughts of dark bouncy curls framing an angelic face that hid a surprisingly strong character. Thoughts of a slender body clad only in a blanket, the material following curves his fingers itched to touch, and long legs that he had envisioned, more than once, wrapped around his waist as he drove himself inside her.

Cursing, he stood and threw the pen down on the desk. It was only understandable, he reassured himself, that he was entertaining thoughts of himself and Rosalind tangled up in his bed. It had been well over a year since he'd had sex.

Was that why the attraction he was now feeling for the feisty and determined lawyer was so strong? So all-consuming.

He stalked to the window. Not only did he want nothing to do with her damned envelope full of papers, with resolving his father's estate, but he also wanted—no, *needed*—to keep his distance from her and the temptation she presented. Jumping into bed with a woman he'd just met would be repeating his past sins. Placing pleasure above more important things like taking up the reins of Lykaois Shipping.

Or serving out his punishment for the way he'd lived for the past thirteen years. Focusing on hedonistic pursuits and material goods instead of maintaining a relationship with a father who had experienced his own loss.

A punishment that seemed all the more just when he allowed himself to remember how things had been before Elizabeth Lykaois's death. Yes, he'd been raised in luxury, traveling frequently between his mother's native England and his father's home in Greece. But he'd never once doubted his parents' love, had been secure in a way he knew few children were. He'd been drawn to the finer things in life. Belen had even cautioned him about his preference for new cars and dating around in his first couple of years at university. The tone then, however, had been one of paternal warmth, of sharing words of wisdom with a boy turning into a man.

Not the cold disappointment that had followed as Griffith had spiraled out of control after Elizabeth's swift illness and shocking passing. Once he started, once pleasure eclipsed anguish, it had been impossible to turn back.

And every time his father had reached out, every time Griffith had been tempted to sit down and have a heart-to-heart with his father, he'd backed out of it, unable to bear it. His father had represented love, family. Things that demanded he open his heart and deal with his pain.

So he'd run. Run in the opposite direction and welcomed anything and everything that would distract him. And ignored, to his detriment, the small part of him that wanted to reconnect with his father. To grieve with his father.

A part he now realized he should have paid more attention to.

His lips twisted into a grimace. It was awful to have a life-changing realization after it was too late to do something about it.

Griffith glanced out the window at the gardens. They had been his mother's pride and joy. When one of his father's solicitors had shared the real estate listing for the chateau, his mother had fallen in love with it. The black gates had been rusted and falling off the hinges. The roses had grown wild, tangling over the sidewalks and up the walls. The mosaic in the grand hall had been chipped, some of the tiles missing. Even then he had been drawn to the modern, the contemporary, seeing more value in the designs of the future rather than getting stuck in the past. His father had been a mix, appreciating aspects of both history and the future. But his mother, while she had appreciated innovation, had been in love with history.

Nowhere was this more evident than in the chateau and all the loving work that she had put in to restoring it to its former glory. The year before she'd gotten sick, she had spent almost every waking hour at the manor, working alongside bricklayers and restoration specialists, learning the craft and pouring in as much of her own blood, sweat and tears as she expected from the workers.

At the time, he had been proud of her, with her dust-covered face and big happy grin as she stood in a pair of overalls. She'd held a paint roller in one hand and a glass of wine in the other as she'd celebrated the completion of the painting of the great hall with her husband and son.

Yet as his grief had taken over after her death, he'd come to resent the chateau. It had started small at first, wondering if she hadn't been so caught up in the resto-ration if she might have noticed the little signs of her ill-ness sooner. Then his father had invited him down to tour the finished home just a few months after the funeral. It had been too soon. He had declined, seen the hurt in Belen's eyes. By not going, he had started a snowball ef-fect that would affect his relationship with his father the rest of his life.

But he hadn't been able to bring himself to step a foot back into the house that he associated with her. The house that should have brought joy and instead only served as a reminder of what would never be.

It had been around that time that he had thrown him-self into what his father had described more than once as a self-indulgent lifestyle. The never-ending carousel of trips, luxury cars, yacht parties and one-night stands. By the time he'd hit thirty and realized that his way of life could only be sustained by buying more, doing more, to fill the always present chasm his mother's death had carved out inside him, he hadn't known any other way to exist.

And, he admitted to himself as he stared out the window at the roses, now tamed and flush with summer beauty, the thought of trying something new, of putting effort into overcoming his grief, had seemed insurmountable.

*Coward.*

A movement caught his eye and tore him out of the past. Rosalind walked down the steps of the patio and into the garden. She wore a creamy blouse tucked into a dark blue skirt that circled her waist and fell in soft folds past her knees. He did a double take as he realized that her feet were bare.

When he had realized that she had no clothes except the dress she'd worn, he'd gone up to the attic. His mother had never been able to resist supporting aspiring artists and designers, ranging from painters and sculptors to aspiring fashion moguls. Many of them had found their success under her patronage and had sent her gifts, including their own work, as thanks. He had recognized the label on one of the trunks, now an international fashion powerhouse. Knowing his mother had never even seen the garments had helped him steel himself against the sudden onslaught of emotion.

Also knowing that Rosalind would be wearing clothes instead of that damned blanket had helped as well.

She wore them well, he thought as he watched her move about the gardens, wandering along the stone path, stopping here and there to smell a flower. Casual, but elegant, they brought out her natural beauty. Her curls lent her a youthful air. But the confident set of her shoulders, the delighted smile on her face as she smelled a rose the same pale orange as the sky at dawn, made him all too aware of the fact that she was a woman.

She ran one finger over the petal of a rose. The sight made him hard in an instant.

*You're a grown man, not a prepubescent teenager.*

His body ignored the lecture from his rational mind as blood pumped through his veins. He should turn away, needed to get back to work.

*One more second. Just one.*

She stopped, frowned. Threw one last look of longing at the flowers before she moved back to a table on the patio and sat down with a sheaf of papers. Working, no doubt. Trying to figure out how to convince him to sign those damned papers.

The woman wouldn't know how to have fun if it bit her.

*You could show her.*

No, he couldn't. That part of his life was over.

The sound of a chime drifted up through the open window. He saw her glance at her phone, could sense even from here the sudden tension that gripped her. The occasional phone call or text message would still occasionally slip through.

Who was reaching out to her? Her boss? Her parents? Perhaps a boyfriend? Just the thought of another man talking to her, kissing her, touching her, filled him with an unexpected pulsing rage.

Cursing, he turned away from the window and went back to his desk. Was he so desperate for connection, so starved for physical affection, that he had taken to spying on a guest, no matter how unwelcome she was? To creating imaginary lovers to vent his frustration and anger on? Succumbing to jealousy, an emotion he'd never experienced before?

He managed to refocus on a proposal from a board member about expanding their shipping routes to include the Northwest Passage the following summer. A move that would save ships currently navigating through the Panama Canal thousands of miles, not to mention time, fuel and money.

The proposal, well written and well-thought-out, drew him in. So deeply engrossed was he in reading that it took him a moment to realize someone was knocking on his door.

He looked up just as the door swung open. Rosalind stood in the doorway. Her fingers plucked at her skirt as she hesitated on the threshold of the room he'd told her to avoid.

Shocked that she would defy a direct order, furious that she had done so, he remained seated. Let the silence stretch between them.

"I…" A deep blush crept over her cheeks. "I need to speak with you."

"I told you to stay away from my office."

"I know. I—"

"But you decided to invade?" He stood then, a thin thread of humor beneath the quiet anger in his voice. He slowly circled around the desk like a predator stalking its prey. "Trespass? Ignore any and all common decency because you wanted something and damn anyone else who might get in your way?"

She swallowed hard as he prowled toward her. But she didn't back down. He hated that he liked her for that. Hated that even with fury pounding through him he noticed details he shouldn't, like the swell of her breasts pressing against her shirt, the rapid pulse dancing at the base of her neck.

"I need to talk to you."

"So you said. And I told you I had no interest in speaking to you."

Her eyes narrowed. "Did you ever stop to ask me what I wanted? Or do you just toss out orders and expect people to obey them without question?"

"Yes."

"That's not how I operate, Mr. Lykaois. I talk to people, ask them what they want, engage with them."

"Then you're in the wrong business, Miss Sutton."

Her lips parted as something flickered in her eyes. She glanced away, then back at him so quickly he would have missed it if he hadn't been looking right at her.

"I'm good at what I do."

He walked back around the desk, put much-needed distance and a physical barrier between them.

"Apparently not good enough."

Instead of bursting into tears or responding with fiery words of her own, she merely cocked her head to one side and pinned him with that mossy green gaze that saw far too much.

"Does it work for you?"

"What?"

"This impenetrable shield you've got going on."

She stepped closer. The muscles in his back tensed. Suddenly he felt cornered, with the windows at his back and fiery temptation in front of him.

"You snap at people. Say horrible things to push them away." Another step closer. The faint scent of jasmine reached him, teased him with its alluring dark floral fragrance. "But I think there's something else going on."

"I didn't realize you had a degree in psychology, too."

"No, just good people skills. You keep people at arm's length because then you don't have to try."

His mouth dried. "Excuse me?"

"When you're rude to people, you set a precedent. No need to try, no need to make nice when people don't expect it of you. Then you can hide in your Kent estate or your secret London club or wherever and just…" She threw her hands up in the air, as if trying to physically grab onto the words that eluded her. "Just wallow in your pain and misery."

"Wallow?"

If she caught the dangerous edge to his voice, she didn't show it as she held his gaze.

"Yes. I lost my mother a few years ago. I know it's hard to move on from—"

"You know nothing."

He ground the words out, watched as her eyes widened in alarm. She saw too much, made him want too much, feel too damned much. She had the perception, the power, to rip away every wall he'd built and leave him with nothing except the pain he'd managed to keep at bay for thirteen years.

She threatened his very sanity. He needed her gone, out of his office, out of his life.

Now.

"Don't try to build a bridge between us, Miss Sutton. There is no common ground. Yes, we both lost our mothers. But that is where the similarities between us end. If you think sharing the *woe is me* details of your life will somehow make me sign that contract, then think again."

*Too far.*

He'd gone too far. She didn't cry, didn't yell, didn't

even blink. But he could feel the change in the air, the cold creep in as her heart hardened against him and his reckless words.

Ashamed, his eyes flickered to the side, caught sight of his reflection in the glass of a painting hanging on the wall. The scars twisting down his face, distorting his once handsome visage into something unnatural and beastly.

*Monstrous.*

That was what Kacey had called him. And she was right. The way he acted could be monstrous. But how else could he protect himself?

"No, I don't know your whole story, Mr. Lykaois, or what losing your mother was like." The compassion beneath her cool words only deepened his guilt. "I think you're punishing yourself." A board creaked. The scent of jasmine grew stronger, sweet yet seductive. "But have you ever stopped to think, for even one moment, that you're punishing everyone else around you, too?"

It was as if someone had reached down his throat, wrapped their hands around his lungs and squeezed every ounce of air from his body. He couldn't speak, could barely think, as the shocking weight of her words penetrated and left him adrift in a new reality.

One where, once again, he had made himself the center of it all.

He recovered just enough to say what he should have said the moment she came to his office door.

"Get out." The icy calm in his voice belied the storm raging inside him.

With the faintest rustling of her skirt, Rosalind turned and did exactly that.

# CHAPTER EIGHT

ROSALIND PAUSED LONG enough to pull on a pair of slippers she'd brought downstairs before she hurried out the door onto the patio. Heart pounding, eyes aching with unshed tears, she rushed down the stairs and into the garden.

She'd gone to Griffith's office to bring up the contract again. She knew it was wrong, knew he'd told her to stay away. But a text Mr. Nettleton had sent yesterday had come through, demanding to know why she hadn't sent him a daily report. It hadn't been too hard to imagine the barrage of missed calls, texts and emails that would be waiting for her when she finally got back into an area of full service. It had galvanized her to action.

The last two days had been spent distracting herself with work, reviewing documents she had thankfully packed in her briefcase for the new clients she would take on after she completed the Lykaois contract. She had told herself she just needed to give Griffith time to adjust to her being at the chateau. That one day she would come down and he would at least be in the hall, the kitchen, somewhere other than hiding away.

This had marked the third morning she'd come down to an eerily empty house. Nettleton's text, combined with her exasperation over Griffith's immature behavior, had spurred her on as she'd climbed the stairs to the third floor. It had been long enough since their last encounter over the contract. Surely, he could take five minutes and listen to his options.

Except he hadn't. And then he'd been cruel. Like a wounded animal lashing out. His pain touched her empathetic nature, tugged at the strands of her own grief of losing her mother.

But it had also done what he'd intended it to do. Hurt her until she had no choice but to turn away before she let him see just how deeply his words affected her. How his insinuation about her career path chipped away at her already eroding self-confidence. How his accusation that she would use her mother's death to connect with him and entice him to sell struck at her heart.

As she walked down the path, she glanced to her left. A small tunnel of ivy beckoned to her, curving just a few feet ahead so she couldn't see what lay at the end.

Needing something, anything, to distract her, she stepped inside. Coolness enveloped her as the thick netting of ivy shut out the sunlight. She followed the twists and turns of the tunnel, running her fingers over the thick, smooth leaves.

Slowly, she became aware of a dull roaring. Anticipation built as the sound grew louder and the ivy began to thin. She turned another corner, saw the sunlight up ahead and, beyond that, the beautiful blue of the sea.

She emerged onto a plateau thick with wild grasses and flowers. Wind rose up over the nearby cliffs, tumbled across the plain and stirred the stalks of grass into a frenzy.

Mindful of the cliff's edge, she walked until she was twenty feet or so away from it. Being unfamiliar with the terrain, she had no desire to end this eventful journey with the ground suddenly giving way and falling into the ocean.

A glimmer of white caught her eye. Turning, her breath caught.

A couple kilometers down the coast, the ocean curved into a shallow bay. The plateau jutted out far enough that she could see a sandy beach backed by soaring white cliffs and topped with green grass. The cliffs nearest to her jutted out into the ocean and formed an arch. Beyond that, at the far end of the beach, a single pillar of white jutted up from the waves, the top narrowing into a point.

The setting from the painting. Even though the painting had been stunning, it didn't hold a candle to the view in front of her.

It was odd to see the cluster of buildings beyond that. To know there were people so close and yet so far away.

Her lips curved up. Even if she lost her job, lost the respect of her family and friends back home, she would have moments like these to remember from her chaotic adventure. Moments that made her feel…content. Peaceful. Like herself.

She wrapped her arms around her waist. If the worst happened and she did lose her job, the hardest part would be telling her father. It had been her parents' dream for her to go to college, to travel and see the world. Since Rosalind had entertained those dreams herself, it hadn't bothered her much that her parents had been so adamant about certain things. Her ability to find the good had helped, too. Even when something hadn't felt quite right, had felt more like a wish of her parents' rather than her own, she hadn't known what she wanted enough to take a different path.

But now, as she faced the truth that she wanted something far different than what her parents had envisioned for her, she was also confronting the very real possibility of letting her father down. Of seeing his face crumple as he realized his daughter wouldn't be a powerful attorney at a distinguished law firm in London. That she might very well own a hole-in-the-wall office helping single parents and grandmothers instead of wealthy CEOs and political powerhouses. Barely scraping by but being fulfilled by the good she was doing.

She'd never disappointed her family before. Didn't want to.

But she also didn't want to keep living like this. Working hard, then harder, then harder still, all for something far in the future and missing the present.

She glanced back at the chateau, at the numerous gleaming windows and polished stone. The kind of place she would have described as a fairy-tale castle.

Right now, though, it seemed little better than a gilded prison.

A shudder passed through her. If Griffith Lykaois wanted to hide here from the media attention, that was his choice. He was punishing himself. For what, she had no idea. The news reports had all stated that Griffith had had a green light. That the driver, whose blood alcohol level had been triple the legal limit, had torn through the intersection and only applied the brakes a second before the crash.

His mother had passed from some sort of illness. Something also out of Griffith's control. Yet based off the articles she'd read, his indulgent lifestyle had started a few months after his mother's death.

She sighed. Slid off the flats she'd found in the trunk

and savored the feel of cool earth and soft grass beneath her bare feet as she'd chosen to in the rose garden earlier. It grounded her, gave her a moment of much-needed pleasure as her mind tried to piece everything together.

None of it was her business. Just like going into his private domain had been none of her business, she realized that. Yes, she'd been angry. And growing bored. But there had been books scattered throughout the house. Other rooms she could have explored. Garden paths she hadn't ventured down. A beautiful kitchen with plenty of food and ingredients. She had chosen work, as always, over taking time to relax, to do exactly what she had been saying she wanted to do and enjoy herself.

And then she had given her dratted boss even more power by letting his text get to her and spur her to action. Instead of waiting, of hanging out in the kitchen or one of the main rooms Griffith would have to pass through eventually, she'd violated his request and intruded on his privacy.

She sighed. Four days to go. If she left Griffith alone, gave him space the next few days, perhaps by the time the bridge was repaired they would both be in better places to at least have a conversation about the contract.

*You're in the wrong business...*

Had he seen how much those words had twisted her up inside? How much they'd torn at her rapidly growing doubts?

No, she wasn't good at working with clients like him. Big clients with big reputations and even bigger bank accounts, the kind who brought prestige to a firm like Nettleton & Thompson. She preferred working with the grandmother who wanted to divide up her assets fairly among her grandchildren. The parents who worried about providing for a son with health concerns once they passed. The husband confronted with his mortality too soon who wanted his wife and children to be financially stable.

Those were the people she wanted to work with. The people she loved working with.

Once she became a midlevel attorney, those types of clients would be rare. Even rarer still when she became a senior attorney.

A bird flew overhead. She watched it soar, swoop down before it arced back into the sky. Entranced, she stepped forward as it winged out over the edge of the cliff and flew above the waves.

"Stop!"

Startled by the loud voice behind her, she whipped around. A sharp, stabbing pain shot through her foot as something pierced her skin. She sank down into the grass, clutching at her leg.

"What in the hell do you think you were doing?" Griffith demanded as he reached her side.

"What are you talking about?" she asked as she gritted her teeth against the pain.

"Do you have any idea how unstable the ground is around here? How close we are to the cliffs?"

"Yes," she groused as she looked down and spied a thorn sticking out of the sole of her foot, "dangerous territory."

"If you hadn't come traipsing about out here, you wouldn't have gotten hurt."

"If you hadn't ordered me to get out of your office, I wouldn't have been out here in the first place."

He dropped down next to her and took her foot in his large hands with a surprisingly gentle touch.

"If you hadn't come into my office when I told you not to, I wouldn't have asked you to leave."

Her lips curled back over her teeth as another bolt of pain shot up her leg at his probing.

"You know, I think I have something that trumps all of this."

He arched a brow as he glanced up. "Oh?"

"If you would have just signed the contract or the refusal, we wouldn't be in this position right now."

He stared at her for so long she wondered if he was just going to leave her out amongst the grasses. Instead, he did something even more unexpected. He scooped her into his arms, held her tight against his chest and stood.

"What are you doing?" she shrieked.

"Carrying you back to the house."

She thumped a hand against his chest. "Let me down. I can walk."

"Not with a thorn that size in your foot."

"Hobble, then," she amended.

"I'm more than capable of carrying you."

Through her pain she detected the offense in his tone.

"I'm not saying you're not physically capable," she said quietly.

His hold on her tightened. It startled her, made her want to relax into his embrace, savor the novel sensation of being carried by a man who obviously took good care of himself.

*Dangerous.* The warning whispered through her mind. Griffith, and her attraction to him, were very dangerous. She had never got to know a man well enough to feel comfortable taking a relationship beyond a good-night kiss. Thought that was what it would take to want to take things further.

Then Griffith had appeared in her life. She didn't know him at all. Comfortable was the opposite of what she felt when she was around him. The instantaneous attraction was both thrilling and overwhelming.

Yet it had also set off warning bells. How could something so sudden be real?

No matter what she felt, he was off-limits. Yes, technically his father's estate was her client, not him. But Griffith was involved. Sleeping with him could derail the career she'd worked so hard for.

Satisfying a simple burst of hormones was not worth that risk. It couldn't be, could it?

The rest of the trip back to the house was made in silence. Once inside, he took her into the kitchen and sat her down on one of the chairs. She watched as he moved about from the state-of-the-art refrigerator and freezer hidden behind wood paneling to a cupboard that contained stacks of neatly folded cloth.

"How does it feel?"

"Painful," she ground out through gritted teeth.

He sat in the chair across from her and made a motion with his hands for her to bring up her leg and rest it on his knee. She did so, even though it stung her pride.

"Hold still."

"I'll try."

"If you yank back, I may not be able to keep a hold on it and it could break off in your foot. It could cause an infection."

"I have three brothers. I helped my mom patch them up enough times to know about pulling out things. Thorns, glass, porcupine quills."

His lips lifted a fraction. Not much, but just enough to count as an almost smile.

"Porcupine quills?"

"It always amazed me," she forced out as pain pulsed in the bottom of her foot, "how something with such a cute face could be so menacing."

"I've wondered the same thing."

Her eyes came up to meet his and she realized with a jolt of surprise that he was teasing her.

"You're saying I'm cute?"

"Perhaps."

Shock rendered her speechless. He thought she was cute? She would have preferred beautiful or sexy. But she could make do with cute, too, especially from a man like him who maybe offered a compliment once or twice a year.

"I think the last time I was called cute," she finally managed to say, "was in middle school by Henry Dorsey."

"And you and he didn't live happily ever after?"

"My brothers scared him off. As they—"

With a sudden yank, he pulled the thorn out of her foot.

"Ouch! You could have warned me."

"Which would have made you tense up and made it all the more likely that the thorn would have broken off in your foot."

She managed to keep her lips pressed together as he cleansed the wound and wrapped her foot.

"Thank you."

His head snapped up. "What?"

"Thank you," she repeated. "For taking care of me."

He blinked, as if he didn't know what to make of her gratitude. His lips parted, then came back together before he finally managed to say, "You're welcome."

Tension still lingered between them, but her accidental

sojourn into the wild rose bushes had created a temporary truce between them.

A truce she needed to avoid. A truce meant the potential for her attraction to him to flourish. To tempt her closer to crossing a boundary she needed to keep in place.

"There."

He lowered her foot to the floor, then stood up and moved away from her quickly. Relieved, she braced her hand on the table and started to stand.

"What are you doing?"

"Going up to my room."

*And as far away from you as I can get.*

"Don't put pressure on that foot, at least not for a few hours. It was a good-size thorn and it's likely to be pretty painful."

"Okay," she said slowly. "If I'm going to be off my feet for a couple hours, I'd rather not do it in the kitchen. Besides, as I said, before I'm very good at hobbling. I can make my way upstairs—"

He moved forward. She started to step back, winced as her foot made contact with the floor. The pause gave him enough time to sweep her into his arms once more.

"Or I could just carry you."

"You've really got to stop doing that."

"What? Playing Prince Charming?"

She threw back her head and laughed. When he glanced down at her one brow raised, it only made her laugh harder.

"Not handsome enough for Prince Charming?"

"Oh, it's not that," she hastened to reassure him. "You're actually too handsome."

He shook his head slightly. "Too handsome?"

Embarrassed, she looked away.

"You said it."

"I wish I hadn't."

"Why not?" he asked as he walked out into the main hall and headed toward the stairs. "Say more if you like. I haven't heard a compliment about my appearance in... well, you can guess," he said with a sardonic smile.

"What else is there to say?" She could feel the heat creeping up her neck and moving through her cheeks. "You're handsome."

"Handsome enough to be Prince Charming?"

"Yes," she practically growled.

It was his turn to chuckle, a sound that hummed in his chest and stirred her skin. As the pain in her foot resided, she became aware of how snugly he held her body against his, of the sheer strength in his arms as he gripped her tight. She snuck a glance at him from beneath her lashes, her eyes traveling over the sculpted line of his jaw beneath his beard, the scar that cut down the left side of his face.

"Ask."

"Excuse me?"

"The scars." His lips thinned into a line. "Everyone stares, but no one has the guts to ask."

What would it be like to have everyone know the details of your life? To know almost every horrific thing and still want to know more, to take every bit of knowledge as if it were their own?

"I didn't really have a question. More of an observation."

"What's that?"

They reached the top of the stairs. As he moved down the hall, he spared her a glance.

"That it's very unfair that people won't leave you alone."

This time his laugh was short, harsh. "For once, Miss

Sutton, you and I agree. I didn't used to mind the spotlight. As I'm sure you know, I embraced it."

She thought back to the hours of meticulous research she had performed preparing to accept this challenge. To try and get inside the head of Griffith Lykaois, renowned shipping magnate and consummate playboy.

"I know."

He reached her room and walked in through the open door, then sat her down on the long midnight blue sofa in front of the fireplace. As he released his hold on her, she knew a sense of loss, one that affected her body as much as it did her heart.

He moved over to the fireplace, turned his back to her as he braced his arm against the mantel.

"You think me spoiled."

She thought for a moment, tried to find a way to be diplomatic. And then decided that the best course was truth.

"Yes."

"I am," he replied simply. "I'm spoiled and I like nice things. I also have the kind of money that can buy the kind of things that attract a lot of attention. Coupled together with…" He gestured at his face. "What I used to be, it attracted a lot of attention."

She frowned. "That's not all everyone focused on. I read a number of articles about the advancements you and your father made—"

"Stop." The order snapped out, wiped away any of the intimacy that had developed between them in the kitchen. Her body tensed as she watched the tightening of muscles in his back beneath his shirt, the cords of his neck tensing.

"Don't talk about my father. Please."

"Okay."

She wanted to say more, to offer some sort of comfort.

His behavior, everything he said, convinced her more and more that while he might have selfish and indulgent tendencies, the man in front of her was a man in pain. A man with hidden depths, given the level of care he had administered to her just minutes after their argument.

He faced her then. Sadness bloomed in her chest at the frozen expression on his face. The mask had slipped back once more.

"Can I bring you anything?"

"No. I had some of the frozen crepes and fruit for breakfast. And there are bottles of water here in the guest room."

One corner of Griffith's mouth quirked up. "Beatrice lives in constant hope that one day I'll return to the chateau. Bring someone here who I could share it with."

A vision filled Rosalind's head, of Griffith in the rose garden, a baby bouncing on his knee, a toddler running about. It was hard to imagine any of the women she'd seen pictured on his arm out here amongst the historic elegance. They seemed more suited to the city, to the nightlife and luxury shops that abounded in cities like London. But Griffith... Surprisingly, she could picture him here.

"Well, when you see her, please thank her."

The stilted conversation stole her remaining energy. She leaned back into the couch.

"You could use some rest." Griffith inclined his head to her. "I'll check on you later."

"I should be able to be up and about on my own in a few hours."

"I'll check on you all the same."

"You would have made an excellent doctor," she said as she failed to stifle a yawn.

"I sincerely doubt that," he replied dryly. He hesitated, then nodded his head, as if he'd made a decision. "Tomorrow."

"Tomorrow?"

"We'll talk about the contract."

Confusion cut through her fatigue. Why the sudden change of heart? Had her accident stirred up some emotion? Perhaps guilt?

*Does it matter? Just say yes!*

"Okay. Thank you."

He nodded once more. "Get some rest."

As she shifted down to stretch out on the couch, she heard his sharp inhale, turned her head to see what he was about to say. But he was moving toward the door, not even looking in her direction. She waited until the door clicked behind him before she let her eyes drift shut.

Never in a million years would she have pictured a man like Griffith tending to her. It had made him seem almost human. And, she thought as she drifted off to sleep, it made her attraction to him all the more treacherous.

# CHAPTER NINE

GRIFFITH KNOCKED ON Rosalind's door the following morning. He steeled himself when he heard her footsteps, stayed strong when she opened the door wearing a navy blue shirt and a vivid red skirt, her curls caught up into a loose bun that left her neck bare to his gaze.

Then lost his grip as he imagined trailing his lips from jaw to shoulder, then lower still—

"Good morning."

"Good morning."

Rosalind blinked and stepped back at the growl in his voice. He started to explain, then stopped. He just needed to get this conversation over with. When he'd suggested it yesterday, the offer had been rooted in guilt and curiosity. Guilt for the way he'd treated her not just the past few days, but the past few weeks. Curiosity about the woman who didn't give up, who couldn't let herself enjoy more than a few moments in a rose garden.

Who made him crave not just sex but something more. Something that carried a power he'd never experienced before.

Dangerous. Yet so tempting he couldn't resist spending just a little bit of time with her.

Chances were these few minutes would finally relieve

him of some of the attraction he felt. Take away the mystery, the anticipation, and he would be left with a beautiful woman who wasn't a good match and, after this week, would be out of his life for good.

That was his plan. And that plan should not be unsettling him as much as it was.

"My office."

She blinked at the command in his voice, but simply nodded. He turned and walked out. A moment later he heard her footsteps behind him. If he was going to do this, to concede to her and listen to something that threatened to rip out what was left of his heart, then it would be in the one place in this massive house he felt in control.

He gestured to a chair in front of his desk as he circled around and sat. She leaned over and handed him a thick bundle of papers in a leather folder before taking her seat.

"Your father's estate is currently valued at approximately one billion, four hundred million dollars."

A number Griffith had aspired to for years. To officially wield the title of billionaire. A number that, as he opened the folder and stared at the figure, stirred nothing but sorrow. Sorrow that his father had worked so hard while spending the last years of his life widowed and estranged from his only child. Sorrow that Griffith had been the reason for that estrangement.

"I have my own fortune." He closed the folder, set it down on the desk. "I don't need the money."

"You have several options. You can accept the estate in its entirety. You can accept part of it. You could reject it all."

"What happens if I reject it?"

"Then it goes to the next family member. A distant cousin living in Greece."

He frowned. He knew the cousin she spoke of, a decade older than him with a predilection for alcohol and drugs.

He sighed.

"So I have no choice."

She tucked a stray curl behind her ear. "May I make a suggestion?"

"I'm surprised you even asked."

She arched a brow at him. "I read a lot about your family when I was assigned your father's estate—"

"Why were you assigned to it?" Griffith interrupted.

"Excuse me?"

"This is a rather high-profile account for a junior associate to take on."

She sighed. "It is. My boss had it. When you declined to meet with him for so long, he put it on me, too. I think he thought I could either succeed where he hadn't or, if it all fell apart, he could blame it on me. Either way he gets the win."

Disgust slithered through him. "And you never get any of the credit."

"He's brilliant when it comes to law. Unfortunately, he only cares about the law as it benefits Nettleton & Thompson." She looked at him then and narrowed her eyes. "Back to the estate. Your parents were both involved with a number of charities and start-ups."

"Yes. My mother invested quite a bit of her time and money supporting independent artists, fashion designers, photographers."

"And your father, if I remember correctly, financed scholarships for underprivileged youth in his home country of Greece."

"He grew up extremely poor. My grandfather founded

Lykaois Shipping when my father was a teenager. He started off as a dockhand and worked his way up."

"You must be proud of them." She glanced at the papers, then back at him. "What causes are important to you?"

He blinked. "What do you mean?"

"Causes," she repeated. "You know, charities, philanthropies."

"I maintain donations to all of the charities and trusts my parents set up."

A wrinkle appeared between her brows. "Is there nothing you care about personally?"

Uncomfortable with the direction the conversation was taking, he shrugged.

"I continue to support the causes my parents championed. I ensure alterations to match inflation. I'm not capable of more."

She frowned. "Not capable or you don't want to open yourself up to more?"

He flashed her a cold smile. "Monsters aren't capable of giving much, Rosalind. I give money. That's my limit."

Her frown deepened. "You really believe that, don't you?"

"Yes." He pointed to his scars. "Inside and out."

"I don't believe that."

The quiet conviction in her voice hit him. Made him, for the first time in years, want to be something more than the shadow he'd turned himself into. Drifting in and out of life, marking time until it was all over.

More temptation. More yearning. He didn't want to end their time together just yet. But he couldn't stand one more moment of talking about the damned contract. Talking about his life and all of his failings.

"Let's talk about you."

Her eyes narrowed as her nose wrinkled.

"Me?"

"Yes. You intrigue me. Tell me more about Rosalind Sutton. The woman who let her boss walk all over her without question."

She shrugged as a pale blush stole over her cheeks.

"Not much to tell."

"What do you do for fun?"

"I work a lot." Embarrassed, she stood and started walking around the room. Pacing like she was caught in a trap. "Sometimes I read."

"Fairy tales?"

That surprised a small laugh from her. "Sometimes. I do love the happier ones. Romance and cozy mysteries if I'm not reading briefs or final testaments."

"What about family? You mentioned three brothers."

"They're wonderful unless they're being terrible," she said with a grin. "Always looking out for me."

"What about your parents?" Too late, he remembered what she had said about her mother. "Disregard that."

"It's okay." She smiled at him, a truly kind smile meant to reassure. "It happened so fast."

"Were you able to be with her?"

"I was in Chicago at school. I didn't make it back in time."

She swallowed hard, grief evident in every subtle gesture, every slight movement of her body. Never before had he been so in tune with someone, read every single one of their emotions. Grief, regret, a lingering sadness. It all echoed his own. Everything he never allowed himself to feel, never allowed another soul to see.

"But you came back to England?"

"I did. My parents were very proud of me getting the internship. When my mom heard about the job offer, my chance to live abroad..." She looked back at him and smiled. "I don't think I ever saw her so excited."

"What about you?"

"What about me?"

"Were you excited?"

She blinked, as if she'd never been asked such a question before. Irritation flickered inside him. She spoke about her family in glowing terms. But what kind of family relentlessly foisted their own dreams on their children? His parents had made it clear that his path forward would be his own. His father had told him multiple times that, while he enjoyed the idea of his son taking over as he had done for his father, it was always Griffith's choice.

"I mean, yes. Not many people make it out of the small town I grew up in, let alone all the way to London."

"What about your work? Did your parents push you into that, too?"

She scowled. "They encouraged me to get a degree and move out. Take advantage of opportunities they didn't have."

He dialed back his frustration. If it didn't upset Rosalind, it shouldn't upset him. Only it did. It bothered him that everything she'd worked for, everything she should be proud of, came second to her parents' happiness.

"And you chose law."

"I took a career exploration course my first year in college. I enjoyed the legal unit we did and excelled at math, reading legal documents. A professor recommended I look into estate planning." She smiled. "And here I am. I like helping people, and the stories they bring into my office. They're interesting. Helping them navigate that stage of life, and giving them peace of mind to enjoy the rest of their days. Never something I saw myself going into when I was younger, but I really love it."

"And you like working for Nettleton & Thompson?"

There it was. That same flicker of emotion he'd witnessed down in his office when he'd lashed out at her.

"I do."

"But?"

"Sometimes the prestige… I'm just not always sure that Nettleton & Thompson is the place I'm meant to be."

"Then why continue with it?"

"Wanting to see it through. I promised my parents I would." Her fingers traced a circle on the surface of the table. "Maybe I'll do something else later. Open my own firm."

He heard the faint, dreamy note in those last words. Started to ask more, but she interrupted him.

"Anyway, back to business. What if you donated your father's estate? Contributed to causes they believed in, and some that you believe in, too?"

He sat back in his chair. She sat up straighter, squaring her shoulders as if readying for a fight.

"I'm not talking about the contract. I'm just pointing out that you seem removed from everything in your life. Let's take you right now, in this moment, with a wealth few have. Why don't you find something you care about? Something personal? Donate the estate so you don't have to worry about it, but do something good with it, too?"

"I had something I cared about," he shot back. "Now it's gone. I do the bare minimum, which when it comes to my personal situation, still means millions of dollars every year getting funneled into charities and organizations around the world, not to mention paying some of the highest salaries in the shipping industry. Take the stars out of your eyes, Rosalind. I do more than enough with what I have. Just because I don't get my hands personally dirty doesn't lessen the impact I'm making."

"Perhaps if you were to get more involved, you could find something else you care about."

"Why are you pushing me on this, Rosalind? Surely, this is beyond your legal duties," Griffith warned her. This conversation was taking a turn he had never intended. Had not permitted. And yet, she still persisted.

"I don't know you," she admitted. "But I see a man who has so much potential, that could be so much."

"Because I'm rich?"

"It's not just about the money. There's this whole other man beneath the harsh exterior, but you've got him locked away so deep down inside that I don't think even you know who he is. Maybe you did once, but not anymore."

The accuracy of her statement hit home. Anger welled inside him as he stood, his chair scraping against the wood.

"And what about you, Miss Sutton?"

"What about me?"

"Do you know who you are? Or are you simply the woman everyone else wants you to be?"

Her lips parted, closed, then parted again as she stared at him.

"What?" she finally gasped. "I just told you how I went after my career—"

"Yes, at a school your parents pushed you to. A job you accepted because it would make your parents happy."

The more he talked, the angrier he became. He was a lost cause. But this woman, so full of life, so full of potential, was wasting it all on someone else's dreams. The anger also helped to restore his sense of control. Anger he understood, an old friend that kept his heart guarded and hurt at bay.

Except once again, she didn't turn around and walk out. Didn't capitulate or surrender. She faced him, fierce and furious.

And gorgeous. Gorgeous with her eyes snapping emerald fire and color high in her cheeks. Her determination had drawn him in that day at the Diamond Club. Now it harnessed his anger, fanned the fires of his fury into something hotter.

Her eyes darted down, rested below his waist. The blush deepened as her chest rose and fell. He saw the blink, the sharp intake of breath, the desperate attempt to regain control of her own desire.

Seeing the naked lust in her gaze yanked him back to that edge. But right now, with his blood roaring and his body pulsing, the boundaries didn't seem like something to avoid. No, he wanted to take her in his arms and hurtle over the edge, wrapped up in each other.

Her tongue darted out, touched her lower lip.

"Sometimes we do things for people we love." Breathy, husky, her voice wound through his veins, a siren's song he could no longer resist. He took a step toward her, his body thrilling when she didn't retreat.

"I wouldn't know."

"Surely you must have loved someone once."

"Once." He stopped just inches away, stared down into her eyes. "Not something I plan on repeating."

"When you love someone, you'll do something for them even if it's not what you want for yourself."

He leaned down, left a whisper of space between their lips, imagined he could hear the frantic beat of her own pulse as she tilted her head back. The seduction came naturally, a skill he hadn't used in what felt like ages, but that was easy to summon.

The desire, however…that was beyond his control. And right now, he didn't give a damn.

"I'll take your word for it, Miss Sutton."

With that pronouncement he laid a hand on her waist, the other sliding into her hair as he tilted her head back farther still. He heard her sharp intake of breath, felt the warmth of her skin beneath his hands.

And then his lips met hers and his world exploded.

For a moment she didn't move. When she came alive, he knew he'd made a mistake. She didn't shy away, didn't pull back and call him a monster.

She returned his caresses with a fervor he hadn't anticipated, couldn't get enough of. Her lips pressed against his. He reached up, pulled at the band securing her hair and thrilled to the feel of curly silk cascading down, a strand whispering over his scarred cheek, his neck. She trembled as his hands moved up and down over her arms. When her fingers threaded through his hair, tugged, he groaned. His hands moved to the waist of her skirt, pulled the hem of her shirt free. He touched the bare skin at her waist, knew he was lost when just brushing her with his fingertips brought him to the edge.

His tongue slipped inside her mouth, deepened the kiss. Her answering moan, the way she met him with strokes of her own, drove him mad.

His hands slid higher, over her ribs, his knuckles grazing the silk of her bra.

He wanted it gone, wanted to touch her bare skin.

He reached around, fingers settling on the clasp. It wasn't until he heard her whisper his name, felt the eager press of her body against his, that it hit him just what he was doing.

Stunned by his loss of control, he pulled back so quickly she stumbled. She stared at him, eyes wide, breasts rising and falling as she sucked in a shuddering breath. One hand drifted up, as if she were moving through a dream, her fingers settling on her swollen lips. With her shirt wrinkled and her curls pulled free of the bun, now hanging in wild disarray about her face, she looked ravished. Seduced.

Aroused.

*No.* Her wanting him, returning his desire, was the last thing either of them needed.

"Griffith…"

He shook his head. "Rosalind… Miss Sutton… I'm sorry."

"No…" Her eyes were wide, luminous.

Wanting.

"Don't be sorry."

Her breathy voice curled around him, smoky seduction and tantalizing temptation.

It also had a surprising effect on Rosalind. She blinked, as if waking from a trance. Her fingers wrapped around the top of her chair. Something primal inside him howled, reveled in the effect he had on her even as he hated himself for surrendering to his base instincts.

She bit down on her lower lip. "I… I have to go."

She grabbed the leather portfolio off the desk, turned and walked out.

*Oh, Theé mou.* At least *she* had come to her senses. That would make keeping their hands off each other easier over the next few days.

*Liar.*

It made nothing easier. Now that he'd tasted her, felt her answering passion, his need had become so intense it physically hurt.

How long could he spend with Rosalind before he dragged her down, too? Took that beautiful, optimistic light and squelched it with his own selfish needs and grief?

*Is it worth the risk? Worth hurting someone else, hurting her?*

He knew the answer. Knew the answer and hated it as much as he hated how he had very nearly lost control.

He moved to the bank of windows behind his desk. The gardens behind the house lay before him in all their glorious summer splendor. Roses swayed back and forth in the breeze. The benches and archways scattered throughout, providing havens for readers, explorers and lovers.

He turned his back on the gardens. Refocused on his office, the sanctuary of his own company, even as he ignored how his footsteps echoed off the walls and amplified the void inside his heart.

# CHAPTER TEN

ROSALIND SAT CURLED up in a burgundy wingback chair in front of a massive stone fireplace, a book lying on her lap. She could imagine it filled with burning logs in the winter, fire crackling over the wood as thick snowflakes fell outside.

She'd tried, and failed, several times over the morning to focus on work. After realizing she had read the same page of a client profile four times and not retained a single word, she'd shoved the papers into her briefcase and made her way to the library.

Every creak, every little noise, had made her heart pound. She had no idea what she would say to Griffith when she saw him again. She should apologize for her glaring lack of ethics, her unprofessional behavior.

Except she didn't want to. For so long she had been pushing her own wants and needs to the side. Had thought in the beginning that she needed to keep her attraction to Griffith buried, convinced that giving in to someone like him would only leave her heartbroken, would take her focus off work.

She had told herself to stay away from Griffith on a personal level. To keep her attraction to him in check. But the more she contemplated a future without Nettleton &

Thompson in it, the more she thought about breaking off and finally going after something she wanted, the less she worried about the professional implications sleeping with Griffith would carry.

And the more she imagined his body on top of hers, what it would feel like to be filled by him, to have him move inside her...

Her skin tingled at the memory of his lips on hers, the way his hands had slid into her hair, exuding strength and yet such exquisite tenderness it overwhelmed her. She'd surrendered without a second thought.

An affair between them wouldn't lead to marriage. Of that, she had no doubt. They moved in different worlds. He was determined to keep everyone away.

But he obviously found her attractive. What if, she wondered as she closed the book and got up, they could come to some other arrangement?

The idea of an affair, of having a man like Griffith introduce her to sex, excited her. But it wasn't something to be taken lightly. She'd always thought the first man she'd sleep with would become her husband. This was very much not going to be that.

Taking a moment to let her chaotic thoughts settle, she wandered about, taking in the details of a renovated eighteenth-century library. From the soaring cases fashioned out of dark, gleaming walnut to the windows that stretched up three stories high, it was truly the personal library of her dreams. Luxurious, brown leather chairs were arranged about the room. Two sofas and two love seats, the color of a deep, fine wine, had been placed in the middle of the room on top of a plush Persian rug. The faint scent of wood polish, coupled with the fragrance of old books, was almost a seduction in itself.

Which brought her right back to Griffith. To the glimpses of the man he was beneath his pain. The feelings he stirred inside her. The way he desired her, like she was a craving he couldn't satisfy. It made her feel beautiful, empowered, alive.

*Think this through.*

Irritated at her mind's less than enthusiastic response, she grudgingly trudged back to her room, even though every cell in her body screamed for her to go upstairs and tell him. Ask him to be her first.

She felt no fear. No second thoughts. Only desire.

But was it worth it? Mixing something so intensely personal with the biggest contract of her career? Worth sharing her body with a man she knew she had no future with?

With her nerves on edge and her body unsatisfied, she needed to do something to relax. She had touched herself before. But as one friend had once so depressingly put it, it had been the equivalent of scratching an itch. Short, hurried sessions that had always left her frustrated and feeling vaguely disappointed.

But not tonight. No, tonight she was embracing the passion Griffith had awakened in her.

Slowly, she unzipped her skirt, imagining his hands on the zipper, fingertips grazing her back as the material parted. The skirt pooled at her feet with a sensual whisper of fabric that sent a delicious shiver over her skin, followed a moment later by her shirt. Her hands came up, cupped the weight of her breasts as she closed her eyes and let her head fall back.

What would it be like? To have his hands on her, teasing her, stroking her? Her eyes drifted shut as her fingers grazed over her own nipples, a gentle touch that teased them into hard buds and made her breath catch. Would he be gentle, tender? Or would he take charge, pushing her to the limits of what they could both handle as he dominated her body?

With a languid sensuality winding through her, she moved into the marble bathroom and turned on the claw-foot tub's hot water. A black end table standing next to the tub offered an assortment of soaps and a bottle of rose-scented bubble bath. As steam drifted up, she poured herself a glass of red wine from the minibar, pulled a plush robe from the closet, and found a box of matches in one of the drawers. Minutes later, she sank beneath the bubbles. A candle flickered on the counter. She'd dimmed the lights, creating a dreamy atmosphere that seduced almost as much as the desire she had finally surrendered to.

She took a fortifying sip of wine before setting the glass down on the window ledge next to the candle. Leaned her head back on the plush pillow at the back of the tub. Then let her arms drift down below the surface of the water. One hand wrapped around her breast, squeezed gently, tugged. The other moved lower, over her belly and down to the apex of her thighs. Her fingers stroked the sensitive skin, up one side and down the other, before lightly resting on her clitoris. She pressed, gasped at the sensation that spread, an electric current that lit up her entire body. Her mouth curved up into a shocked smile as she continued to tease, touch, exploring herself in a way she never had before.

Her passion built. Her hips arched against her own hand. Even as the pleasure spread, too, it made her acutely aware of the ache between her thighs. Images of Griffith filled her head, the thunderous expression on his handsome face before he'd crushed his lips to hers, the way his scent had wrapped around her as he'd kissed her to the point of madness on his desk.

"Oh, God…"

She found her release, stronger than she'd ever experienced before. But the pleasure did nothing to assuage the ache Griffith had stirred in her.

She sighed. Even if Griffith said no, she wasn't going to head back to London and go in search of a random one-night stand. No, she needed some kind of connection to make that leap. And she sorely feared that, after the incredible desire Griffith had stirred in her, she wasn't going to find anyone like him ever again. Even someone who could offer her all of the future dreams she eventually wanted.

She breathed in. Exhaled. Thoughts swirled in her head, some louder than others, all of them chaotic and demanding attention.

Through the storm, one constant remained.

She wanted Griffith.

Her thoughts quieted. Peace reigned even as anticipation made her pulse beat faster. She wanted Griffith to be her first lover. She wanted everything she'd experienced these past few days: the excitement, the passion, the tenderness mixed with a primal lust that nearly made her come apart in his arms.

She dried herself off, applied a minimal amount of makeup, and contemplated the dresses in the trunk. What did one wear, she thought with a wry twist of her lips, to ask someone to take her virginity?

Settling on a simple sleeveless black dress with a V-neck that teased a peek of her cleavage and a full skirt that swayed just above her knees, she moved out the door with a confident set to her shoulders. This time, as she climbed the stairs to the third floor and walked down the hall to his office, it wasn't dread that pounded through her veins. There were no thoughts of contracts or inheritances or promotions.

Only Griffith.

She knocked on the door. A moment passed. She knocked again.

Dimly, she heard footsteps. Then the door swung open. Griffith stared at her. She returned his gaze with one of her own, taking in the tousled hair, the long-sleeved tan shirt and dark pants that followed the lines of his muscular physique.

"Why are you here, Rosalind?"

"Because I want you."

He blinked. Once, twice.

"What?"

"I want you, Griffith." Her heart climbed into her throat as she pushed herself to the edge of her limits, reached out with both hands for something she wanted with a desperate passion. "I want you to be my first lover."

He stepped back, his face contorting with shock. "First?"

She silently cursed herself. "That didn't come out right."

"Either you're a virgin or you're not, Rosalind?"

Intrigue dripped off every word.

She tilted her chin.

"I am."

He let out a melodic string of Greek, the harsh sting of his tone making it clear he was cursing.

"A virgin?" he repeated.

"Yes. I understand we're a rare breed past a certain age, but it does happen."

He turned away, groaning as he scrubbed a hand over his face.

"Rosalind, I need you to leave."

"No." She stepped forward, planted herself in the doorway so he couldn't slam the door in her face. "I won't go away unless you look me in the eye and tell me you don't want me, too."

"That's exactly why you should go away." He turned on his heel then, stalked back across the room until a mere whisper separated them. "Because I want you. I want you so badly I ache for you. It physically hurts not to touch you."

Her chest rose and fell, desire twisting and twirling through her veins with such ferocity it made her feel faint.

"Then why not?"

"Because that's all I can offer you." He stepped back then. "Physical pleasure. With whatever time you have left here. Nothing more."

"Did I ask for more?"

His raspy laugh sounded torn from some place deep inside him. "Not now. But a woman like you, Rosalind, you shouldn't even have to ask. A man should look at you and know that you deserve more than one night. More than a few pieces of jewelry."

Her lips parted in shock. It meant something that Griffith saw her like that. Despite her insistence that this would only be a physical thing, she knew that she was risking, and would most likely lose, part of her heart to this man. This man so convinced of his own hideousness that he couldn't see the moments where his humanity shone through.

Was it worth it?

*Yes.*

"And I want those things. Eventually. A husband. Marriage. Kids. But not right now."

His hands tightened into fists at his sides. "You know the twisted part about all of this? Just the thought of you being with someone else, sharing your body with another man, makes me want to rip his head off." He looked away. His sharp profile caught in the light streaming in through the windows. "But I can't give you any of that, Rosalind. I'm not capable of offering anyone that kind of emotional depth."

"And I'm not asking for it."

"You should." He placed his hands on her shoulders, his fingers tightening on her skin. "You should ask for the world, Rosalind. You should not settle for what you think you can get because you're stuck out in the middle of nowhere with a man who can't control his own lust. Look at me."

He craned his neck to the side so that she could see the full scarring along the side of his face. He grabbed the collar of his shirt and yanked down, revealing the continued path of the scars as they snaked down his neck.

"Do you know what my ex-girlfriend said when she first saw me in the hospital? 'Monstrous.'" He released the collar, let the fabric creep back up over his scars. "And she was right."

Rosalind stared at him, her heart aching.

"Then she wasn't the right woman for you."

Griffith threw back his head and laughed, harsh and grating.

"Obviously."

"I said it before, and I'll say it again. There is nothing repulsive about you."

"Then perhaps you haven't looked close enough. You

said you loved fairy tales. Don't most of those talk about the beauty within? About the importance of who someone is on the inside?" He moved toward her. "I do not have any beauty within. There is no love in my heart. I am not capable of it."

"I'm not looking for love. Not with you."

Did she imagine the flicker in his eyes, the flash of something dark?

"You're just looking for a quick lay to finally see what sex is all about?"

"Not too quick."

Instead of lightening the mood, her quip made his eyes turn molten. He swallowed, his hands clenching, unclenching.

Sensing that his resolve was weakening, she moved forward, savoring the burst of feminine power that wound through her as he watched her with carnal hunger.

"I want you to be my first lover. I've never felt this way before, Griffith. Never wanted someone like this before." She stopped in front of him, slowly leaned up on her toes and brushed a kiss against his mouth, felt him shudder even as he kept himself still.

"I need time to think."

Thrilled that she had at least gotten him to reconsider, she stepped back.

"All right. I'll be in my room."

She had almost reached the door when his voice rang out.

"Rosalind." She turned back. "Could you truly accept an affair? Just an affair? No strings, no emotional attachments?"

She hesitated. There would be no coming back from this. She would be crossing a line, not just professionally but personally. Already she knew there was more to her attraction to Griffith than simple physical lust. She was courting danger, risked her heart, risked everything she had worked her whole life for.

Once she did this, once she gave in to indulgence and put her career on the line, would she ever be able to go back to life as she'd known it?

*But I don't want to go back to how things were.*

"I know you make me want. I want things with you I've never wanted with another man. I want you so much I…"

Her voice trailed off as self-consciousness chilled her ardor. His eyes darkened.

"You what?"

*Be brave. Bold. Confident.*

One more moment of hesitation. And then she stepped off the ledge and flung herself into fantasy. She raised her chin. "I touched myself and imagined it was you."

A growl emanated from his chest, rumbled up his throat as his jaw tightened.

"This is my choice, Griffith. I choose you. I hope you'll accept that."

*"Mori."*

The word sounded torn from deep within him. And then he was in front of her, sweeping her into his arms as he kissed her with that incredible passion that sent flames licking over her skin and a deep, pulsing need straight to her core.

"I'll be damned tomorrow." His voice rumbled against the sensitive skin just below her jaw as he trailed his lips down her neck. "But tonight, Rosalind…" His hand tangled in her hair as it had the first time he'd kissed her, arched her head back and bared her throat to his mouth.

He knew just where to kiss, to nip, to drive her wild until she was panting and wet.

"Tonight," he repeated as he brought his lips back to hers, "you're mine."

# CHAPTER ELEVEN

HOW HAD HE ever thought her straitlaced? Buttoned-up? Because the sensual creature in his arms was anything but staid. She moaned, gasped, met him touch for touch as he explored her with his lips and tongue.

She'd touched herself. Thought of him while bringing herself pleasure. Despite his scars, what he'd shared, she still wanted him. Her desire for him, coupled with their undeniable chemistry, stripped away the last of his misgivings.

He leaned down, slid an arm beneath her knees and lifted her into his arms. Unlike their adventure out on the plains, where he'd barely been able to resist from tasting her, he now feasted. He carried her next door to his bedroom. He stopped next to his bed, his fingers sliding the zipper of her dress down. When the material pooled at her feet and his hands came up to cup her breasts, he nearly lost it when he realized she was completely naked.

"Rosalind…"

"There wasn't any underwear in the trunk," she said with a smile that turned into a moan as he stroked a finger down the slope of one breast. Her sharp inhale was music to his ears. He kissed her again as he continued

to stroke and touch. He took everything she had to give,
demanded more.

*Selfish.*

And he couldn't stop. The only thing that could have
made him stop was her, and she responded to every touch
with a need that made him so hard it nearly hurt. He teased
the seam of her lips with his tongue. She opened to him,
gasped into his mouth as her fingers dug into his hair.
Pressed her body against him. Deepened the kiss.

He stopped by the bed and lowered her down onto
the silken cover. Reveled in her moan of protest as he
straightened.

And stared.

His eyes consumed the sight of her. The swell of her
breasts. The slope of her stomach, the flare of her hips,
the dark curls, the curves of her thighs.

Her skin, still pink from the heat of her bath, darkened
as a flush spread over her body. But she didn't move to
cover herself. No, his tenacious beauty shifted, slowly
arched her back and looked right into his eyes.

"Are you sure, Rosalind?"

She nodded. The trust she placed in him, the desire
that flamed in her forest green eyes as she looked him
up and down, pierced his armor in one fell swoop. That
she trusted him with something so important, that she
still wanted him despite his scars, touched him in a way
he'd never experienced before, enhanced the desire pulsing through him.

*What if she knew it all? Would she still want you then?*

He pushed those thoughts away. She knew how things
stood between them, that what they were about to do
wouldn't go further than the chateau. When they both left,
that would be the end of anything personal between them.

His fingers closed around the hem of his shirt.

"Wait."

Disappointment felt like a cold fist around his heart. A sensation that disappeared almost immediately as she stood and reached for him, her hands tentative but her eyes luminous. Her fingers settled over his, slipped beneath his shirt and grazed his stomach. His eyes drifted shut as his breath escaped in a harsh exhale. She pulled his shirt off.

Then froze. He uttered a silent curse as he suddenly remembered.

The scars on his face paled in comparison to the marks down his left side. One scar stood out from the rest, an angry slash over his ribs down to his waist. Smaller scars branched out from it, some faded and pale, others more visible.

Slowly, she reached out, laid a hand on the most prominent scar. At his sharp intake of breath, she snatched her hand back.

"Did I hurt you?"

"No." Not even close. Feeling her touch had been... wonderful. A deep part of him wanted to beg for her to touch him, just once more. "No one other than the doctors and nurses have touched me there since the accident."

She reached out again. He held his breath, only releasing it on a harsh exhale when her fingers trailed down over the scar.

"Griffith..."

He tensed. "Yes?"

"I want you."

He kissed her. Raw, sensual, commanding, yet vulnerable, he took everything she offered and demanded more. She gave and gave as his hands roamed over her body, cupped her hips and pulled her tight against his hardness, caressed her breasts until her nipples puckered once more beneath his touch.

Her bare breasts grazed his chest, nearly drove him insane as the light touch stoked him hotter, higher than he'd ever been with a woman.

Then her nimble fingers settled on the waistband of his pants. His eyes flew open and he captured her hands in his.

"But I—"

He kissed her, a deep kiss that coaxed a response with strong, sure strokes of his tongue, which she answered with excited passion.

"If you take my pants off, I may not make it to the bed."

Delight filled her face, giving him another glimpse of the dreamer she'd suppressed for so long.

"You want me that much?"

"More."

He kissed her again, edged her back toward the bed until her knees hit the mattress and she tumbled back.

"Damn it. I don't have a condom."

"I'm on the pill." At his arched brow, she frowned. "I planned on having sex one day. I wanted to be prepared."

He chuckled. "And I've never been happier to hear that. I haven't been with anyone since the accident."

"And I haven't been with anyone. Ever," she added with a naughty grin.

His smile disappeared as he looked at her again, his eyes lingering on every inch of her body.

"Show me."

"What?"

"Show me," he repeated in a voice raspy with need, "how you were touching yourself."

She watched him for a long moment, her beautiful breasts rising and falling, her lips parted.

One hand moved. Fingers trailed over her face, down the curve of her neck to her breasts. When she cupped herself, uttered a soft gasp as she tugged on the hardened peaks, he nearly lost it. He was so hard it hurt.

Then her hand slid lower. He widened his stance, imagined chains wrapped around his ankles keeping him anchored to the floor so that he didn't interrupt this, didn't stop one of the most arousing and beautiful things he'd ever seen. To see a woman like Rosalind, tenacious and intelligent and yet so innocent, take charge of her pleasure entranced him more than he had ever thought possible.

His breath caught in his chest. Desire tightened, squeezed the air from his lungs as her fingers slid into the dark hair at the top of her thighs. Her eyes drifted shut as she touched herself. Her hips moved, her legs shifting restlessly as her breathing grew heavy. He curled his hands into fists even as he moved forward, using his own legs to gently nudge hers apart where they draped over the edge of the bed. Imagined himself sliding into that slick, wet heat. Hearing his name on her lips when he took her for the first time.

*Not yet. Soon, just not yet.*

For nearly a year he had denied himself pleasure. He could survive another minute.

And then she arched up, her moan filling the air between them.

"Rosalind."

She opened her eyes, panted as her gaze moved up and down his body.

"Griffith. I need you."

He shucked off his pants and covered her body with

his. Moans filled the air as his chest pressed fully against her breasts. Their hands moved, caressed. He kissed her mouth, the tip of her nose, grazed his lips over her temple. He trailed his lips down over her cheek, her jaw, her neck, inhaling the faint fragrance of rose that clung to her skin.

Then he shifted, pressed kisses with gentle grazes of teeth along the slopes of her breasts. She cried out, her fingers digging into his hair, as he sucked one tight nipple into his mouth. He wanted more, to move fast, to satisfy himself.

But something else drove him farther down her body, a need to make this moment intimate, special for a woman who had trusted him enough to choose him.

His hands settled on her thighs. He spread her legs, the scent of her arousal making blood roar in his veins.

"Griffith…"

He heard the hesitation in her voice, looked up even as his fingers pressed down on her skin.

"I want to taste you, Rosalind." He turned his head, pressed a kiss to her inner thigh that made her tremble. "But only if you say yes."

Slowly, she parted her legs even more, her fingers trailing over his face, moving with the same gentle caress over his scars and unmarked skin. Her touch, her lack of fear or disgust, made his throat tighten as he lowered his head.

The first touch was a brush of his lips against swollen, sensitive flesh. Her answering moan made him smile. He teased her with kisses and licks and nips along her thighs, the skin just above her mound.

But when he kissed her again, he tasted her desire.

And had to have more.

Gentleness disappeared as he devoured her. Her thighs clamped around his head. Her fingers tightened in his hair as she cried out, urged him on as she bucked against his mouth, incoherent sobs barely registering past the roaring in his ears.

Her body tightened, stiffened. She screamed his name as she peaked before sagging onto the bed.

He moved, slid up her body as he dropped a kiss on her hip, the slight swell of her stomach, the dip between her ribs. She lay still, her breathing shallow, her face turned to one side.

"That…"

"That what?" he prompted.

Her eyes fluttered open. She turned her head and smiled lazily at him.

"That was amazing."

"I'm glad."

He said it with no small degree of masculine pride. But beneath his own satisfaction lingered the tenderness that had surprised him in those first few moments, that had guided his actions as he had made love to her body with his hands and mouth.

Her eyes widened as he moved his hips, his hard length pressing against her thighs.

"Oh."

She shifted, the action making her slick skin rub against him. He groaned, breathed in deeply to steady himself.

"Are you ready?"

She nodded. He placed himself at her entrance. Slowly, he eased inside. Her body closed around him, tight and hot and so wet he nearly came right then. She tensed as he came up against the barrier. He slid a hand into her hair, cradled her head and kissed her as he pushed deeper, swallowing her small cry of pain.

When he was fully inside, he stopped. Let her get used to the sensation of him inside her.

Even if it nearly killed him not to move.

"Thank you."

Her whispered words swept over him. Prompted by a rising tide of emotion, he leaned down, kissed her. The kiss was gentle, warm, affectionate. A chance to savor the moment, the monumental change that had just occurred.

She wiggled. He groaned.

"Don't do that unless you're ready."

She arched a brow as the corners of her lips tilted up. "Do what?" She moved again. Her eyes widened. "I can feel you getting bigger."

"That tends to happen when a man is aroused."

She slid her hands up his back.

"Show me what happens next."

He pulled out, reveled in the shocked wonder in her eyes as he slid back in. He started slow, long strokes that drew out the sensation, gave him the chance to notice things he'd never paid attention to with previous lovers. The flush that spread up from her breasts to her neck, the hitch in her breathing when he sank himself to the hilt.

Their pace quickened. She started to meet his thrusts, her fingernails scraping across his skin as she moved beneath him.

"Griffith. Oh, God, Griffith, I can't..."

"Don't hold back, Rosalind." He kissed her. God, he couldn't stop kissing her. "Do you trust me?"

"Yes."

Pressure built. He couldn't have stopped it if he had tried.

"Then give it all to me. Everything."

She surrendered, her body clamping down on him like

a vise as she came apart in his arms, his name uttered over and over. He found his own release a moment later, shuddering as an intense pleasure wracked his body.

He eased himself down onto her body. Enjoyed the comforting feel of her beneath him, her fingers gliding slowly up and down his back.

For the first time that he could remember, he wanted to stay.

Which was why, after letting himself have just a moment longer, he rolled off and got up.

"Griffith?"

He looked back and inwardly cursed. She lay on her back, her slender body looking even smaller in the vastness of the bed where he had just taken her innocence. Taken an incredible gift, used it and was now abandoning it.

Because he was scared. Frightened of what she stirred in him. What she made him want. He had thought the simple temptation of her was dangerous enough.

But these unexpected bouts of tenderness, of romance, were even more perilous. He needed safety, not risk. Isolation, not emotion.

Except that meant focusing only on what he wanted and needed right now.

*Classic Griffith.*

"I'll be right back."

He went to the bathroom, ran a hand towel under warm water. When he came back, Rosalind frowned, then glanced down at her legs. A blush burned in her cheeks.

"Um… I can do that—"

"Do you remember what we just did?"

"I was there."

Her feisty reply gave him the chance to kneel on the

bed, to slowly wipe away the traces of their lovemaking and her first time.

"You gave me something tonight. The least I can do," he said as he tossed the towel into a hamper, "is give you something in return."

"You did. Twice."

He threw back his head and laughed. "Then we're even."

Her brows drew together. Another curse rose to his lips. He'd been clear about how things would stand between them. But did he have to make their interlude sound transactional? Especially in the moments after she'd just been with a lover for the first time?

"I..."

She stopped. He saw the insecurity flash across her face, the doubt. This was the moment he could break the pattern of holding himself back, and let himself connect with someone beyond a mutually shared pleasure.

Except the words couldn't come. That he had been moved to do something as intimate as care for her after sex, that he was even contemplating inviting her to stay, were signs he needed to reverse course and reintroduce distance between them.

So he said nothing.

"Thank you, Griffith."

Before he could retreat, she leaned over and kissed him on the cheek. A simple action, chaste compared to what they had just done to each other in his bed. But the sweet gesture stabbed deep and wrapped around his heart. Made him want things he didn't want to risk wanting. Things that would require emotion, risk, sacrifice.

She rolled away and stood, plucked her dress off the floor and walked to the door. Did he imagine her hesitation as she grasped the handle? The shudder that passed through her as she turned it?

Then she was gone, the door closing behind her with a soft click. Alone, he leaned back into his pillows, closed his eyes, didn't even bother to keep his demons at bay as they came for him, ripping him apart with guilt and self-loathing.

Yes, she'd asked. He'd given her pleasure, paid attention to her needs and wants because he had wanted to, not simply because of masculine pride.

All things he could argue he did for her that made the situation slightly less horrible.

None of them justified the glimpse of pain he'd seen in her eyes when she'd rolled away from him.

*It's better this way*, his demons whispered. *She'll never want you now.*

# CHAPTER TWELVE

ROSALIND WANDERED INTO the kitchen the next evening. She'd slept well past her usual rising time, a pleasant ache between her thighs. And had stayed in her room for the rest of the day. Not quite daring to leave, not quite knowing what she'd do if she ran into Griffith.

Her emotions were still all over the place.

*You've brought it on yourself.*

Griffith had asked her right before he'd invited her into his room if she could handle a simple affair. He'd been nothing but honest with her about what this was, where it was headed. Yet during their lovemaking, the tender way he'd touched her even as he'd worshipped her body like he could barely stand not touching her, followed by the gentle way he'd cleaned her after… He was a practiced lover doing what he did best.

She knew that. Or at least her mind did. Her heart, however, had other ideas.

"Good evening."

Startled, she turned to see Griffith framed in the doorway. Her heart beat a frantic rhythm against her ribs as she forced what she hoped was a relaxed smile onto her face.

"Good evening."

His eyes roamed over her, as if he was trying to discern what she was thinking. Apparently finding nothing amiss, he advanced into the kitchen. Dressed in a white V-neck shirt and navy pants, he looked ridiculously handsome for someone dressed so casually.

"I trust you've had a good day?"

She smirked at him, dug deep for a confidence she didn't feel. "Very."

His eyebrows drew together. She didn't respond, simply watched and waited. Even if she didn't feel casual and carefree about their time together, she would not show him the turmoil inside her. Partly pride, partly embarrassment.

*Perhaps a little bit of heartbreak, too*, her devious mind whispered.

She saw him hesitate and sighed.

"Griffith, I don't want things to be awkward. Last night was fun, but I'm not trying to stalk you. I just came down for some food."

"I didn't think you were." He nodded toward the refrigerator. "Join me?"

"You don't have to—"

"I know I don't," he said as he moved past her and opened the fridge door. "You're hungry. I'm hungry. Join me."

Put like that, there wasn't a good reason to refuse. The "dining nook," as Griffith had called it, was bigger than the kitchen and dining room in her small apartment put together. Set in a large alcove off the kitchen, the massive windows offered soothing views of the rose garden.

"How do you not spend more time here?"

He glanced out the window. Tension tightened his face for a moment before his expression smoothed out.

"Too far away from my work."

The lie hurt. Ridiculous, she told herself as she speared

a bite of peach covered in zesty dressing. They'd had sex once. He'd made it perfectly clear that after she left the chateau, they wouldn't have anything else to do with each other on a personal level.

Except that when he'd made love to her, there had been moments, numerous moments, when she'd sensed something more from him. A sweetness that had not only relaxed her but also enhanced the experience of sharing her body with a man. An intimacy that had gone beyond the physical and into something that had rocked her to her core.

Perhaps, she brooded as she stared down at her panzanella salad, it had all been in her head. An intimacy born from years of built-up expectations and fantasies concocted from her readings. What had seemed like true love in the dark of night had more than once turned out to be a simple case of lust.

*Not that I'm in love.*

That was ridiculous. Griffith might be an incredible lover. But not only had he made it clear he had no interest in any type of actual relationship, he wasn't the kind of man she wanted to build a life with. Cold, selfish, no interest in a family of his own.

*You had great sex. Let the rest go. Move on.*

She turned the conversation to something she was far more comfortable with: business.

"I saw your company announced your return date next month."

"No work talk." Before she could apologize, he leaned forward. "Tell me more about you."

Flustered, she swallowed, then coughed on the peach. She took a large sip of sparkling wine.

"Are you all right?"

"Yes. Just…not the question I was expecting."

"Why not?"

Now she saw just why this man had been such an authoritative figure in the shipping industry. He could charm someone with that direct gaze of his. He might think his physical scars had marred his features to the point no one would want to look at him. But even with the jagged mark that cut down the left side of his face, the fading nicks and cuts on his cheek and jaw, he was still handsome. Handsome with an innate power that filled a room.

"Um…" She tucked a stray curl behind her ear. "I'm not that interesting."

His eyes sharpened. "You're an American living in London and working for one of the most prestigious firms in estate law. You somehow talked your way into the Diamond Club. You're very interesting."

She barely stopped herself from preening. "Oh. Thank you."

No one had thought her interesting before. Her parents had constantly complimented her hard work and initiative. Her teachers had sided with them, encouraging her to apply for scholarships, to get out of town before she got stuck.

No one had stopped to ask what she wanted. If she was unhappy living in their village by the sea. If she wanted to stay in the community she'd grown up in. Instead, they'd heaped their own unfulfilled and forgotten dreams on her shoulders.

"How did you end up in England?"

"An international internship program. In my second year of law school, we had to secure an internship. One of my professors recommended me for Nettleton & Thompson."

He tilted his head to one side. "You didn't want it?"

"I didn't say that."

"You didn't have to."

She took another sip of wine. She'd never told anyone how she'd really felt as her career had progressed at lightning speed.

*Who better to tell than a man you'll never see again?*

"I was excited about the internship. About living and working in London for a summer. But it was just supposed to be one summer." She smiled slightly. "My mother flew over for a long weekend the summer I had my internship. She was so excited for me." Her smile faltered for a moment. "Probably more excited than I was," she admitted softly, not wanting to meet his eyes. To admit he'd been right. With a quick inhale, she continued. "We crammed so much into those three days. Tower of London, the British Museum, Buckingham Palace. We were supposed to go on the Eye, but it was closed for a private event."

Silence descended.

"What happened to her?"

"An infection. The February after my internship, she caught pneumonia. We thought everything was okay. But four months later she had a lung infection." She swallowed hard. "She didn't make it."

A hand settled over hers. Startled, her head snapped up. Griffith gazed at her with something akin to compassion in his eyes.

"I'm sorry, Rosalind."

He squeezed her hand before releasing her. She took a moment to work past the lump in her throat before she spoke. "I had gotten a job offer from Nettleton & Thompson the month before she passed. Everyone in my town was so excited for me, including my mom. I think because

I enjoyed the internship everyone just assumed I would be equally excited about the job offer."

"But you weren't."

"I just never imagined myself working somewhere like that. Or with clients who could afford a place like Nettleton & Thompson."

"But you didn't want to let your parents down."

"No." She pushed a tomato around her bowl with her fork. "Especially after my mom died, doing something else felt like a betrayal. My parents worked hard to save up for me to go to college."

"What would they have said if you had told them you wanted something else?"

Surprised by the question, she set the fork down and leaned back in her chair. She stared out over the garden, over the silver light of the moon casting a glow over the roses, the shimmer added to the water splashing down from the fountainhead into the pool.

"I don't know. They would have encouraged me to go after my dreams. But," she added as she looked at him, "they would have been disappointed. It sounds so simple. Do what you want, accept your parents might be sad or not fully accept your choice."

"It's not simple."

Griffith's voice whipped out, harsh and guttural. She didn't take it personally. She had a pretty good idea of where his pain lay, of the reason behind his hurt.

"No. It's not simple at all."

"So all work and no play for Miss Sutton?"

"Hard to advance in your career if you're off playing."

"Is that why you are...were," he corrected as one corner of his mouth lifted, "a virgin?"

"Pretty much." She sighed. "I dated. But never long

enough for me to feel comfortable with things going to the next level. And then I just decided to wait until..."

Her voice trailed off. She'd been about to say she had decided to wait until she found a man she thought she might spend the rest of her life with. That wouldn't have gone over well.

"Until what?"

"Until I found someone I was very attracted to."

The look on his face told her he saw right through her lie. But given that he had lied to her about his reasons for not spending more time at the chateau, she shoved her guilt away.

"I don't regret waiting. But I do wish I had... I don't know, lived a little more. Had more adventures."

"Having fun isn't all it's cracked up to be."

The darkness in his tone caught her, stopped her from saying the joke that had risen to her lips.

He trailed two fingers up and down the stem of his wineglass, his gaze turning distant as he retreated into the past. "Indulging for the sake of indulgence. Buying things because they're expensive. Attending parties because of who will be in attendance and not because you want to go." His fingers tightened on the wineglass. He tilted it up, drained the contents, then set it back down with a precision that belied the seething grief and fury she saw in his eyes. "Living in a constant state of working hard and playing just as hard to avoid dealing with something hard."

He leaned back, angled his body so that even though he was looking at her, he physically shut himself off from her. She felt the loss as acutely as if he'd stood up and walked away.

"So perhaps you did yourself a favor. Working hard and staying focused."

The last words dripped with bitterness and self-loathing.

"I doubt someone who increased the value of his family's business as much as you did didn't work hard," she said gently.

"I did work hard. I just played harder. Bought new properties, spent only one night in each of them, sold them the next day. Went to auctions at Christie's or Sotheby's and bought the entire lot because I could. Slept with women whose names I didn't know because they wanted me. Wanted a piece of the millionaire shipping heir, and I wanted sex." His head snapped around, his eyes hard as rock. "Fun is fun until it leads to death. Destruction."

Her heart shuddered, cracked. She wanted to reach out, soothe the anguish from his face and offer him comfort.

A comfort she knew he wasn't ready to receive.

His chair legs grated on the floor as he stood. He collected their plates and carried them into the kitchen. She stayed at the table, turned his confession over in her mind as she watched him out of the corner of her eye.

"Did you always indulge like that?"

A plate clattered in the sink. He stood with his back to her, the muscles in his back tense and pressing against his skin.

"Most of my adult life, yes."

"When did it start?"

"Does it matter?"

He turned then, leaned back against the sink and crossed one leg over the other as he tucked his hands into the pockets of his pants. His broad shoulders, bare to her gaze, slowly dropped, as if he was forcing himself to relax, to appear cavalier.

"I think it does."

He shrugged. "I don't. It was a way of life for me. Now it's not."

"But it still seems to bother you. Like you were living that way of life but not really enjoying it. Like you were doing it for another reason and now regret it."

He pushed off the sink and stalked toward her.

"Maybe I was." He grabbed her hands and hauled her to her feet. "Maybe I wasn't." He looped an arm around her waist, yanked her against his body. "But I can tell you I don't regret last night."

"Griffith—"

"We only have a few days. Let's make the most of it."

The words cut her heart. She knew why he'd said them. To remind her this was nothing more than sex, a short affair that would begin and end at the Chateau du Bellerose.

*Terms you accepted. Terms that were worth both the pain and the pleasure.*

He cut off her next words with a searing kiss that reawakened her desire. She hesitated, then pushed her wavering aside. She'd asked for this. Demanded it. If she only had days to experience this level of need, then she was going to take them and enjoy every single, passion-filled second.

Armed with her newfound confidence, she rose up on her toes, met him this time as an equal as she nipped at his lower lip, drew back a fraction when he tried to deepen the kiss. Glorified in the growl that sounded like it had been ripped from his throat before he took her mouth again.

As his hands slid beneath her bottom, pulled her hips

against him, discomfort flickered through her. Was he using sex to distract her? To keep her attention on the pleasure coursing through her body and off him?

*I can't offer you anything but sex.*

He'd been clear. Laid down the rules. No matter how curious she was, how much she yearned to know him on a deeper level, she had no right to ask more.

With that, she let go of her questions and surrendered to the passion he offered. Let go of thoughts of tomorrow, a week from now, a month. Indulged in the intoxicating sensation of enjoying the now.

Seized by a brazen boldness she'd never experienced, she broke the kiss, slid down his body and dropped to her knees. Satisfaction wound through her as his eyes widened.

Her fingers gripped his waistband and pulled down. When she wrapped her fingers around his length, he shuddered. She stroked him, watched the fire in his eyes burn even hotter as she lowered her head. She took him in her mouth, moaned at the intimacy, at feeling him pulse against her tongue.

She experimented, moving slow and steady, then fast. He hardened, thighs tensing beneath her hands as his head dropped back and he groaned.

"Enough."

He barked the command as he reached down and grabbed her arms, hauled her to her feet.

"I want to be inside you when I come."

Thrilled by his words, by the fever descending over her skin, made all the more potent by their previous intimacy, she didn't protest. Simply gave herself up to his passionate kiss. His hands slid down to her legs, lifted her up.

She wrapped her legs around his waist and moaned into his mouth as his shaft pressed against her still-sensitive flesh through the thin material of her robe.

He whirled around, set her down on the kitchen island. The coldness of the marble served as a sharp contrast to the fever ravaging her body. He kicked his legs free of the pants, pulled the robe up over her hips, and pushed inside her.

"Oh, my God!"

The exclamation burst from her lips as he filled her. He stopped, dropped his head to her shoulder.

She dug her nails into his back. "Don't you dare stop."

He pulled back, thrust deeper as she kissed his neck, his jaw, the scars on the left side of his face. His rhythm slowed.

"Griffith." She clutched his face in her hands, nearly broke at the pain in his gaze. "I want you. All of you."

His fingers dug into her hips. He plunged deeper. She hung on, met his thrusts and arched into him, pressed her lips to his mouth as delicious pressure built, pushed her higher until she couldn't stand it anymore.

"Griffith!"

She came apart on a scream, thrashed as he gathered her in his arms, held her close as he followed her moments later. They soared into oblivion, bound by mutual hunger and a need for pleasure, for connection.

They drifted back down. His breath fell hot and heavy on the tender spot at the base of her neck.

Somewhere deep inside, her resolve weakened, cracked. She couldn't imagine finding a physical connection like this again. But with every tender touch, every time he prodded her for her true wants and desires, saw past the mask she'd worn for everyone else in her life, the more she wondered if she would ever find a man who saw her as intimately and completely as Griffith did.

Not falling for him was becoming harder with every passing hour.

# CHAPTER THIRTEEN

ROSALIND TRAILED HER fingers over the spines of leather-bound books as she explored the second level of the library. After their rendezvous in the kitchen, Griffith had walked her back to her room. He'd left her with a searing kiss.

But he'd still left.

He'd spent the rest of the evening in his office and the night in his room, and she in hers. The way it should be, since they were indulging in a simple, short affair. But she was coming to realize, there was nothing simple about this. The more she got to know Griffith, the more her suspicions were confirmed that his selfish tendencies were not an inherent part of his character. Rather, they were a shield, even a weapon, against the pain of loss.

She hadn't liked the man when she'd first started researching him. But she had respected the professional, the leader who had taken his family's company and elevated it to new heights with strategic decisions and a firm hand. Through the news articles, the occasional interview and, of course, the tabloid stories, she had formed an image of Griffith Lykaois long before she had walked into the chateau.

An image that had been turned on its head when he

had picked her up off the grass and swept her into the house with such infinite tenderness. The bits and pieces he'd revealed of himself since had only strengthened her belief that he was a man who, like so many others, had sought a way to alleviate a deep grief.

He had alluded to his so-called hedonism that first day in his office. Had given her a little more insight last night. And yes, she thought with a wry smile, there had been plenty of photographic evidence of his lengthy and varied dating history. But he had still managed his duties, still led, balancing profits with the well-being of his employees. That had been a source of confusion as she fought through his constant rebuffs.

Now that they had indulged themselves, perhaps they would be returning to their previous arrangement where they stayed out of each other's way until she could return to civilization. A prospect that just only thirty-six hours ago, would have been a relief.

But now it just made her feel unsettled. Even a little sad that her time with her first lover would be so brief.

She pulled a book from the shelf. The soft whisper of leather on leather calmed her, as did the quiet crackling of the spine as she opened the book. The delicious scent of old paper drifted up. Her lips curved as she read the words of the familiar story about a man and a woman determined to keep each other at arm's length despite the passion building between them.

She leaned against the shelf, her fingers tracing over the words. She had been so sure giving in to her desires would send her down the path to ruin. Yet even by the light of day, she couldn't regret what had happened between them. It had been too pleasurable, wonderful.

It had also left her with a sense of languid relaxation

that was carrying her through the morning. Instead of turning her attention immediately to business, she'd enjoyed a muffin on the back terrace, a cup of white tea as she'd strolled through the rose garden, and was now wandering through a massive library instead of reviewing wills, financial documents and lists of personal possessions for other clients.

It was fun, getting to know herself again. To see what activities she was drawn to when she had the rare luxury of a little free time.

A shrill ring cut the silence. Startled, she dropped the book. It took a second for her to realize that the ringing was coming from her pocket. She'd gotten used to the lack of cell reception, the fact that no one could reach her here. Her good mood dissipated when she pulled out her phone and saw who was calling.

"Yes, sir?"

Mr. Nettleton's voice snapped through the line.

"Why haven't you been answering my calls?"

"The reception is terrible here."

"You're still in France? Has he signed?"

"I'm here, but no—"

Before Rosalind could tell her boss about any on the discussions she'd had with Griffith, a squawk of indignation cut her off, followed by a burst of static.

"…no problem removing you from this firm."

Her chest constricted as her fingers tightened around the phone.

"Excuse me?"

"I said I will remove you not only from this case, but from this firm if you don't succeed."

Her heart dropped to her feet. "What?"

"I thought removing the opportunity for promotion

would be sufficient incentive to motivate you to get the job done. Obviously, I was wrong."

Before Rosalind could respond, the call dropped.

Slowly, her hand came down. Blood thundered in her ears as the sunlight streaming through the massive windows turned from a comforting glow to glaring brightness. She sagged against the bookcase, blinking rapidly as she tried to process the bombshell Nettleton had just dropped on her.

Years of hard work. Of pursuing the dream her parents had for her. Of tucking her own hopes away as she'd foregone any type of social life to work harder, do more, be more.

All brought down to one contract the senior partner didn't have the guts to tackle himself.

"Rosalind?"

His voice slid over her, deep and firm, unexpected kindness in his tone. He stood below her, hands in his pockets, his handsome, scarred face tilted up as he watched her.

"Good morning."

"Good morning. Are you all right?"

"I—" She started to tell him, wanted to confide in him. Had always imagined being able to share her life, from the positives to the challenges, with a lover.

But she couldn't. Not when Griffith had explicitly laid out the terms of their arrangement. Even if their relationship was based in affection, how could she put the weight of her career on his shoulders? Whether she liked his decision or not, it was his choice.

"Yes." She forced a smile. "Just an uncomfortable conversation with my boss."

"About the contract?"

She slid the book back onto the shelf, debated how to reply. "About business." She walked down the spiral staircase. "I'll be okay."

She started to walk by him. His hand shot out, closed around her wrist.

"Walk with me."

She shook her head as she tried to pull her hand back. "No, thank you. I've wasted a lot of my morning and I—"

"Wasted how?"

He tugged her closer. Her hands came up, rested on his chest, his heartbeat a steady pulse against her palms. She stiffened and started to pull back. But when he slid a finger under her chin and tilted her face up to his, she found herself holding his gaze. Taking comfort from his presence, despite the intensity of their eye contact. It was as though Griffith was trying to see right through her, into her soul. It was unnerving and exhilarating all at once.

"I've been reading instead of working."

"How dare you?"

His dry comment startled a laugh from her and eased the tension from her shoulders.

"Let's go on a walk. Get out of the house. Clear your head."

"I have work—"

"Do you ever give yourself one day, Rosalind? One day to enjoy yourself."

He took her hand in his, held it with a tenderness she hadn't anticipated, tugged her toward the door.

*I should say no.*

And instead she followed him out into the great hall where they'd officially met for the first time. As he led her toward the front doors, she stopped in front of the painting.

"Where did you find this? It's very well done."

He stared at the painting, his eyes moving over the ridges and edges created by the artist's knife.

"I was at a museum in early spring." He spoke quietly. "An oil painting exhibition. The museum does an up-and-coming artist feature, a booklet where they put together paintings by local artists. I saw this painting and knew it. Knew the style. It had belonged to a painter my mother hosted from Brazil. I dismissed him as an amateur. Even before her death, I had started to gravitate toward wealth. Reputation. Selfishness." His eyes centered once more on the lone figure on the beach. "Buying it seemed like righting two wrongs. Honoring my mother and all the work she did for artists like him. And a way of atoning for how I dismissed him. I had it shipped from Kent when I decided to spend some time here."

Rosalind entwined her fingers with his. He wouldn't listen if she pointed out that the simple act spoke volumes about the man he was becoming.

But she saw it. Saw and knew there was far more to Griffith than he let himself see.

*Maybe one day...*

"It's a beautiful painting."

He glanced down at her. The kiss he brushed across her forehead was unexpected and tender. It stirred something inside her chest, a yearning for more moments like this. Not just the wild, passionate desire they'd indulged in, but times when they just enjoyed each other's company, drew strength from one another as they faced their demons.

*Dangerous.*

The word echoed in her mind once more. But this time, as she followed him out into the sunlight, she felt like the danger Griffith presented was no longer as simple as a threat to her career.

Now he was a threat to her heart.

They walked down the stairs into the bright French sunshine. When he'd notified Beatrice he'd be staying at the chateau, she'd immediately hired over a dozen people from her village to trim the grass, tidy the gardens and clean the house from top to bottom. It hadn't been an insurmountable task. Belen had hired Beatrice to keep the house and grounds maintained when Elizabeth had passed, as if she might suddenly reappear and walk back through the gates. At the time, Griffith had thought it unhealthy at best, a downright obsession at worst. But when he'd driven up twenty-four hours later, he'd been grateful for the cleanliness, the care and attention that had created a peaceful haven. His only thought had been to have nothing to do besides prepare for his return to Lykaois Shipping and savor the silence.

But now, as he and Rosalind walked down the drive, surrounded by velvety green grass, manicured bushes and lush flowerbeds, he was glad she saw the chateau at its finest. As they walked, the tightness eased from her jaw and her usual sunny demeanor returned.

He'd heard enough of the conversation to guess what had happened. And it was his fault. His fault for not being able to sign a damned piece of paper. Before Rosalind had arrived, he'd seen that contract as the last thing standing between him and finally having to accept that his father was truly gone.

He hadn't realized it was affecting more than just him. Not just affecting, he corrected, potentially ruining her career.

Resignation dragged down his own mood. He would

have to have another conversation with Rosalind. A proper conversation about what his options were. Before she left, one way or another, he would have to sign.

He glanced at her out of the corner of his eye. With a slight smile playing about her lips and her bright eyes looking skyward, it gave him a chance to watch, to savor the sight of her happy and content.

When was the last time he had felt happy and content? Had he ever?

He heard her sigh when they walked past the entrance to the lane of oaks, suppressed one of his own when they saw nothing but the felled tree blocking the bridge.

*One more day. Just one more day.*

Their walk took them through the empty fence posts that his mother had one day envisioned as the beginning of a vineyard, through an apple orchard with trees already laden with growing fruit.

They ended up back on the cliff tops, staring out together over the ocean. He glanced down, noticed a smooth, round rock the color of snow.

"Here."

She smiled as if he'd given her all the jewels in the world. "It's beautiful. Limestone?"

"Yes. Same as the cliffs. Although I don't normally find one so smooth."

She slipped it into her pocket as she stared out over the sea. "It's odd to think that on the other side of this ocean is where I grew up."

"Do you miss it?"

"Sometimes." She sighed. "Living in London, though, is a dream come true. My mother loved my father, loved being a mom. But she told me that she wished she would have traveled more, especially in college. Seen more of the world before settling down."

He heard the wistfulness in her voice, sensed the want coursing beneath the surface.

"That's something you wanted, too."

"Yes. It's why when my parents encouraged me to go to college somewhere else and pursue an internship abroad, I didn't question it too much."

"Why not travel more?"

"I should. I just never have the time." She breathed out. "Sometimes I feel like I've put myself into this box. A really tiny box that grows tighter every year. Like I'm giving up on some things I shouldn't."

"Why keep doing it, then?"

"Partly because of ego. When people learn I work for *that* Nettleton & Thompson, or when I hear my father bragging about me or think about how excited my mother was…" Her voice trailed off. "It's hard to let go of having a parent be proud of you. I worry about disappointing them."

An image of his father flashed in his mind, that last look of defeat on his face moments before the crash. The more he thought about that last look, about how different things could have been if he would have let his walls down, just once, the deeper his regret grew.

"I understand that."

She started, looked up at him. "I'm sorry. I—"

"Don't be. Just because I pushed my father away doesn't mean I didn't want his approval." He followed the path of a seagull as it arched up into the sky, then dove down out of sight beyond the cliffs. "I just told myself I didn't want it."

"I tell myself the same thing sometimes." She leaned

her head against his shoulder in a natural gesture that touched him. "I like looking at the bright side of life. But sometimes I think I focus so much on finding the good in a bad situation that I don't realize it's just a bad situation. One I need to get out of."

They stood there, watching the white-capped waves rise and fall in the distance, each ruminating on their own circumstances.

"Life isn't perfect." She sighed. "I forget that sometimes. Try to paint everything as perfect, to find the good so much I don't accept that sometimes things will be hard."

So had he. He'd been so used to living a charmed life that the loss of his mother had devastated him. He hadn't known how to cope. Distraction had become his therapy, indulgence the balm to his pain. No matter that it had to be constantly reapplied, with increasing frequency and excess. It had been better than falling back into the black void he'd lived in for weeks after his mother's death. A nothingness that had pulled him deeper until he'd wondered if he would ever surface.

They returned to the chateau. She thanked him for the walk and started to go upstairs. Even with just a few steps separating them, he felt her loss. It wasn't simple desire but something deeper, something that made him want to spend time with the woman he was coming to know. He'd never wanted someone this way before. It unnerved him. But unlike the affairs he'd conducted before, his feelings for Rosalind felt...healthier. Stronger. Something more than just satisfying a sexual urge.

Something he wanted to explore, to savor in the precious little time they had left.

"Are you hungry?"

She paused, one hand on the railing. "Yeah, actually. I didn't even realize I was until you said something."

"Let me surprise you."

She smiled even as she tilted her head to the side. "Surprise me? With what?"

"That would ruin the definition of *a surprise*."

She laughed. "I suppose it would."

"I'll meet you on the patio in ten minutes."

"All right. I'll just grab—"

He took the stairs two at a time, gently but firmly reached for her hand and stopped her.

"No work, Rosalind."

"But—"

"If you were caught up on absolutely everything and had ten minutes to yourself, what would you do?"

Her lips quirked. "Well, after yesterday..."

"Besides that," he said even as his body went hard. "I'm not opposed to a repeat performance. But food first."

She ducked her head almost shyly. "I would read."

"Then grab a book from the library and a glass of wine from the kitchen and go read on the patio while I prepare lunch."

"Wine?" she laughed. "At lunch?"

"You're in France. A glass of wine at mealtimes, savored with good company, is acceptable."

She reached up, smooth a lock of hair back from his forehead. Her fingers brushed the top of one of his scars. He didn't flinch.

"Thank you."

He made quick work of making, heating and packing food into a wicker basket he'd seen tucked in a cabinet. He added a couple more things before walking out onto the patio where Rosalind reclined on a lounge with a book and a glass of rosé.

"What's this?" she asked with a huge smile as she sat up.

He held up the basket and, for the first time in months, he returned her smile with a genuine one of his own. "We're going on a picnic."

They traipsed back out onto the grassy plain at a safe distance from the cliff's edge. He laid out the red blanket he'd filched from one of the guest bedrooms before setting out the food and the bottle with the remaining rosé. They dug into the salad, enjoying the contrasting flavors of sharp feta with sweet watermelon and cherry tomatoes. The creamy polenta and seasoned shrimp brought about exclamations of pleasure from Rosalind. Watching her enjoy her meal, how she lingered over a bite, drew out a sip of wine, made him think of the countless meals he'd had at five-star restaurants around the world. He couldn't remember one he had enjoyed more than this picnic by the sea.

"That was incredible."

Rosalind lay back onto the blanket, sliding her hands beneath her head as she watched the sky.

"What dishes do you enjoy back home?"

"Lobster is a big one in Maine. Clams. Anything to do with seafood."

"Would you go back home if you didn't work for Nettleton & Thompson?" The thought made his chest tighten.

She hesitated, then finally said, "I don't think so. It was my home at one time. But even though I followed someone else's dream to get here, I really do love London."

"What would you do, then?"

She was silent for a long time. "I've thought about opening my own firm."

"Why don't you?"

She sat up and picked up her glass of wine, swirled the blush-colored liquid inside.

"I worked so hard to get into the international internship program. So many people coveted the spot I got. And when I was offered a full-time position, only a fool would have turned it down. I've learned a lot from them."

"But it's not what you love."

She slowly shook her head. "No. I got interested in estate planning when my mom helped out our elderly neighbor, Mrs. Carr. Her son and his wife had passed away in a car accident, leaving her with full custody of three grandchildren. She was grieving, terrified that she didn't have enough to take care of them, especially because she wondered about how much time she had left.

"Mom and I were over at her house helping her clean an attic room when an estate lawyer came to visit. Local man, nice enough when I saw him around town. He sat down with her and answered all these questions, helped her make a plan and then a plan for the plan." Her lips curved. "By the time he left Mrs. Carr was...peaceful. It was still a horrible situation, but she was able to move forward." She looked at him then, with her hair gilded by sunlight and the smile on her face content. "I realized I wanted to do that. Help ordinary people find peace and enjoy the rest of their lives."

Floored by the depth of her kindness, unsettled by the stark difference in how they fell into their respective career paths, he watched as she looked out over the gardens. Even though his parents had always stressed leading Lykaois Shipping was his choice, he'd slipped into his various roles with little more than his father's recommendation. When it had been time to take over his current position, he hadn't questioned if he would or would not get it. He'd done good work. Hard work. But he was also a Lykaois. He'd expected it.

He followed the direction of Rosalind's gaze. More oaks had been planted around the perimeter of the garden, their leafy tops soaring above the garden walls. Once he'd recovered from most of his injuries and the pain had subsided to a manageable level, work had been a saving grace. A much healthier distraction than how he'd dealt with things before. Even though he'd taken an official sabbatical, he'd kept his eyes on the company from afar, reviewing the data and reports on a daily basis. He'd grown to appreciate the inner workings, the details he'd thought himself master of that, when applied to an international scale, were far more complex and intricate.

Details he was now responsible for. A duty he had not taken lightly. It was, he realized as he watched the treetops sway in the breeze, something good to come out of tragedy. Something he would give up in a heartbeat if it would bring his father back. The money, the prestige, the company, all of it.

But he couldn't. What he could do, however, was continue on this path, one of responsibility and leadership. One he realized he deeply cared about.

His eyes drifted back to Rosalind. To the serenity on her face, the slight smile about her lips. He'd never been bothered to think past the surface, to see light in darkness. But the woman at his side had inspired him to do just that.

Something shifted in his heart. Something deep that he would have to deal with later.

Much later. Not now, not when he was enjoying himself

too much to stop and think and dissect what was going on inside him.

"Your clients are fortunate to have you."

"Some are even grateful."

She laughed when he arched his brow at her. He reached into the basket and pulled out a small container of fudge. When Rosalind bit into a piece, her eyes drifted shut as she let out a moan that shot straight to his groin.

"This is incredible." She looked at him, happiness radiating from her face. "I wish I lived like you did. Turning something simple into this incredibly decadent experience."

Her words hit him. He'd always seen the way he'd lived his life as an escape, a way to keep himself isolated. It was why he'd punished himself with deprivation the past year.

But to hear Rosalind do what she did, find the good in something, unsettled him. Disturbed the way he'd thought about things for so long. Made him remember a time before his mother's death when his parents had also indulged in the finer things in life, albeit in a much more moderate way. But they had instilled in him an appreciation for both the large and the small, the things they had earned and the things they benefited from because of their station in life.

When had he lost sight of that? Bastardized it for his own selfish needs?

"The way I've lived my life is not something to admire."

"Not all of it, no." She shrugged as she took another generous sip of wine. "Doesn't take away the fact that there are good things. I read some of the interviews you gave two years ago. You know your company. The way you talked about operations and some of the things your departments were working on. Not just big projects, but smaller ones, too." She smiled at him. "Unless it has a six-figure inheritance attached to it, Mr. Nettleton doesn't bother to get involved with smaller clients. But you do. I like that about you."

*I like that about you.*

His breath caught in his chest as her words slid through him, warming him with their simplicity and sweetness.

The possibility that he could be the kind of man she saw him as, the kind of man who could live a better life, was something he had never contemplated before and suddenly desperately wanted.

"Thank you, Rosalind."

"You're welcome, Griffith."

Would he ever tire of hearing his name on her lips? The tenderness and heat in her voice as she spoke?

"The first time you called me Mr. Lykaois, I wanted to hear you say my name."

A delightful crinkle appeared between her brows.

"When I called you?"

"The second time," he amended with a slight smile. "In the lobby of the Diamond Club."

She laughed. "When you watched me get thrown out?"

His smile evaporated. He cupped her cheek, his thumb tracing the delicate line of her cheekbone as he stared into her eyes.

"I did. It was wrong. It was selfish."

"Selfish?"

"I needed you to leave."

Her lashes swept down, then back up as she pinned him with her frank gaze.

"Why?"

"The first time I heard your voice," he murmured, leaning over to kiss her forehead, "I didn't think anything of it. I was too wrapped up in my pain, so angry at what you were trying to do, that I didn't pay any attention." He trailed his lips over her temple. "And then I heard you in Lazlo's office. The feisty American who faced off against the guardian of the wealthiest people in the world."

"Didn't get me far."

Her tone was tart, the underlying breathlessness making him smile in pure masculine satisfaction as he dipped his head.

"It caught my attention." He kissed the curve of her ear, scraped his teeth over her lobe and savored the hiss of her breath escaping.

She pulled back suddenly, leaning away as she stared up at him.

"Did you feel it?"

"Feel what?"

"That day. In the Diamond Club. When I looked up at you, I felt…" She paused. A blush stole over her cheeks. "Never mind." She turned away and set her wineglass down. "It's silly."

He hauled her back against him, buried a hand in her hair.

"Tell me."

Blood rushed to his groin as she bit down on her lower lip.

"Like there was a…a connection."

He swallowed hard. The unknown lay before him, shrouded in darkness and pulsing with potential. Potential pain, heartbreak, loss.

But then there was Rosalind. Here, now, alive and vibrant in his arms, looking up at him with desire and hesitancy. He'd put her through so much these past few weeks. And still she put herself out there, risked his rejection, with more bravery than he had mustered in over a decade. Admitting that she hadn't been alone in what she'd been feeling that day. That it had shaken him to his core, that he had escaped the country because of it. Admitting that would be his own act of bravery.

"I felt it, too."

Her eyes widened. Before she could say anything, he surrendered himself to his desire and took her mouth in a kiss.

Griffith slanted his lips across hers, swallowed her moan of pleasure. His hands moved over her, pressed against her back and urged her closer. Her fingers moved over his face, over his scars.

He tensed.

She grabbed his face in her hands. His own came up, covered hers, the intimacy of his palms on her fingers driving her wild.

He moved so quickly he startled a gasp from her as he eased her back onto the blanket.

"Griffith—"

He kissed her again, claimed her with deep, possessive strokes of his tongue. Her murmurs of delight, his answering moans of passion, fed her, slipped into her veins and heated her blood.

And then there was nothing but sensation, pure and unadulterated sensation as her head dropped back and he set his lips to her jaw. He kissed his way down to the hollow of her throat, laved the sensitive skin with his tongue as she moaned. His fingers undid the buttons on the bodice of her dress, pulled the material down and divested her of her bra with one quick move.

"Not fair." She nodded at his shirt. "You're overdressed."

He grinned and stood, yanking his shirt, pants and briefs off, tossing the clothes somewhere onto the grass before he rejoined her on the blanket. She pushed herself up onto her elbows and stared at him in the sunlight. His well-defined muscles, from his toned arms to his chiseled abs, spoke to the physical discipline he held himself to.

And the scars that covered the left side of his body, trailing down over a muscular thigh all the way to his ankle, spoke to the trauma he had overcome, and survived.

*Griffith*, her heart cried out, *do you not realize how incredible you are?*

She stretched out a hand. He pressed her down onto the blanket as he kissed her again. His lips moved farther down, over the swells of her breasts and her taut nipples, sucking first one rosy peak and then another into his mouth. She cried out, arched against him as he drifted lower still, pulling the hem of her dress up and groaning when he realized she wore no underwear.

He placed his mouth where he had just a day ago. He coaxed her to new heights of pleasure with long, leisurely kisses that drugged her body and sent her spiraling toward pleasure.

She peaked, cried his name. Went limp.

Then came alive again as he moved up over her body. She felt his hardness probing her most intimate flesh. Instinct had her parting her thighs, running her hands up over his back as he pressed inside her. He moved, long strokes that built her up and made her soar. The warmth of the sun, the soft kiss of the wind on her bare skin, the sensualness of making love in broad daylight, all of it heightened the incredible pleasure of Griffith moving inside her, claiming her with every thrust. Sensation built, so bright it was almost painful as she reached her peak. She cried out his name, felt herself come apart as he groaned hers.

And knew as he cradled her close that she had lost her heart to the man who called himself a monster.

# CHAPTER FOURTEEN

SUNLIGHT WOKE HIM. Rosalind's warmth pressed against his side, one arm thrown across his chest and her curls spilling over his shoulder.

He breathed in her scent, allowed himself the luxury of running his fingers through her hair, gently gliding down her back. She murmured in her sleep and her arm tightened around him. The gesture struck him squarely in the heart.

He'd awoken next to lovers before of course. But never had he looked down at their sleeping faces and felt such contentment.

Rosalind's lashes lay dark against her cheek. Her lips were slightly parted, her breathing heavy and even. Satisfaction curled through him. Given how many times they had made love the day before, exploring each other's bodies, indulging the desires they'd both fought for days, he was surprised that he had awoken refreshed and alert.

Especially after their final interlude on the balcony in his room as night had fallen. They'd spent the rest of the day lounging on the blanket, dozing beneath the sun and engaging in another round of lovemaking. By the time they'd returned, the sun had been setting.

As they'd eaten, she'd asked about the third floor of

the chateau. He'd taken her up and given her a tour of the sectioned-off attic, along with his office and his private chamber. He'd shown her the incredible view from his balcony and left her there to go downstairs for another bottle of wine. He'd returned and gone hard at the sight of her naked as she leaned against the railing. The smile she'd shot him as he'd walked out had been daring with a touch of shyness. The intoxicating mix had pulled him in. Instead of leading her back inside, he'd slid his fingers into her curls and anchored her head as he'd plundered her mouth, drinking her moans like a man dying of thirst.

Then he'd turned her around, placed his hands on her hips, and slid inside her. He'd nearly come right then as she'd pushed back, taking him deeper and embracing the wildness of their lovemaking beneath the moon.

Just as he had embraced the connection between them, surrendered to the temptation to show his feelings of tenderness.

When she'd started to roll away, he'd reached out, grabbed her wrist and pulled her back against him. Wide-eyed, she'd stared at him as he'd cupped her face.

"Stay."

He couldn't think of a more beautiful sight than the sweet smile she'd given him before sinking back down against him as he'd pulled the sheet over their naked bodies.

Now she stirred again, murmured something in her sleep, and curled tighter against him. He smiled slightly as he leaned over to kiss her forehead before climbing out of bed. As he walked toward the bathroom, he glanced back over his shoulder. She had already moved to the middle of the bed, arms and legs splayed with her face buried into a pillow. His body stirred at the curve of her bare back, the slope of one naked thigh tangled in the sheets. With the glow of morning lighting the room and her soft snores, he couldn't remember the last time he'd felt this content. The last time everything had seemed perfect.

He froze.

She did look perfect. Here, in his room, in his bed. In all his years of sleeping with women, he had never brought one back to his bedroom. He'd made do with guest rooms, the sofa, even a hotel room. But his bedroom had been his private sanctuary.

Yet he'd brought Rosalind up last night without a second thought. Because he had wanted her to see the view from the balcony. Had wanted to worship her body in the space he felt most comfortable. Safe.

Had wanted more than just sex.

He took a quick shower, turning the water to arctic. The cold momentarily knocked some sense into him, long enough to get dressed and slip out instead of sliding back into bed with Rosalind and pulling her into his arms.

At first, he wandered down the drive aimlessly, eyes roaming over the estate. When his parents had first bought it, he'd enjoyed coming here, watching the house evolve under his mother's dedicated care and his father's bottomless bank account. It hadn't been his style; even though he hadn't fully descended into his hedonistic lifestyle, he'd preferred modern and contemporary.

And after his mother's death…anything that reminded him of her had been too painful. Looking ahead, to the future, had kept him from delving too deeply into what had been.

Yet now, as seashells crunched softly underfoot, he felt a new appreciation for the chateau. That the estate had withstood the tests of time—war, human capriciousness and greed—touched him in a way it never had before.

Because of Rosalind.

He blinked and glanced back at the house. The suite he'd taken as his was on the back side of the house. He wouldn't see Rosalind in one of the many windows, wouldn't see the balcony where she'd arched against him and cried out his name as he'd shuddered and come apart inside her.

With her, he felt freer than he had in years. Even when he'd indulged his wants and vices to excess, when he'd wallowed in his precious possessions, there had been a chain about his neck. With each purchase, the satisfaction had been fleeting. If he waited too long to go out and seek the next best thing, the ache would start. Dull at first, but quickly growing until grief flirted at the edges of his mind and threatened to pull him under.

So he'd bought more, each purchase delaying the inevitable reckoning of his mother's death.

After his father's death, his desire for things had evaporated. The one thing he had desired above all else—to see his father again—was out of reach.

But now, when he asked himself what he wanted above all else, the answer was immediate and clear.

*Rosalind.*

As he neared the entrance to the lane of oaks, he scrubbed a hand over his face. He'd known her less than a week. Had spent the first two days avoiding her entirely. Their sexual chemistry was explosive, their conversations engaging. And she was an incredibly beautiful woman.

*It's more than that.*

Impossible as it seemed, he had developed something that went far deeper than simple affection for Rosalind.

A woman who challenged him, pushed him, yet also supported him in ways no other woman in his past had.

He cared about her. He cared very much.

*You care for her too deeply.*

He *was* in too deep. He'd overstepped a boundary of his own last night by bringing her to his room. Had told himself he could keep his emotions back, that sleeping with her would get this obsession out of his system.

Except it hadn't. The longer he was stranded here, the more time he spent with her, the more he risked wanting what he couldn't have. At some point, he would falter. Would make a mistake and drag her down. His track record when it came to managing and processing grief was abysmal at best.

He hadn't tried to lift himself out of his misery for his own father. Why did he want to now? Because his connection with Rosalind went beyond sex, because he truly cared about Rosalind? Or was he tired of living in his self-imposed state of isolation?

Could he even answer that question? Did he want to? He'd spent a lifetime punishing himself, eschewing emotion and connection. He didn't know how to sustain either. And he knew he couldn't have Rosalind without those, it wouldn't be fair to her. Wouldn't be fair to a woman who craved both.

The sound of a saw cut into his thoughts. His head snapped up. Realization hit him hard in the chest before he rounded the corner and entered the shadow of the oak trees. At the end of the lane, a crew worked diligently to cut up the once mighty tree that had been felled by the storm.

Chateau du Bellerose would soon rejoin the outside world.

He didn't know how long he watched. But as a path

was finally made for a smaller truck to drive through, he started walking toward the bridge. Each step reverberated through him, pushed the thoughts and possibilities that he'd been considering back as reality set in.

Cocooned out here in their own slice of heaven, it had been easy to enjoy her, to indulge her, to allow vulnerabilities to show and secrets to be shared. To imagine himself the kind of man she dreamed about. The kind of man he wanted to be, both for her and for himself.

But that was here. Not London, not the everyday where the demands of life would tug and pull at them. How many people had he known who had jetted off to a romantic getaway, convinced they'd saved their relationship on the white sands of the Caribbean or the lush forests of Bali, only to return to reality and realize that there wasn't really anything left to save?

*We could give it a little time.*

He could hear Rosalind's voice in his head, picture her wide, hopeful eyes. A part of him wanted to do just that. Give whatever they'd started here some time and see if perhaps he was ready for something more.

The image in his head altered, changed to Rosalind with tears glistening on her cheeks. At some point, his selfishness would rear its head again. He'd revert back to his old ways when things got hard. That was just who he was. He couldn't contemplate dragging out what they'd started here when he knew he couldn't give her what she wanted.

He knew what he had to do. Knew what the right decision was.

Knowing that didn't lessen the pain that clenched around his heart and twisted as he turned to walk back toward the chateau. But he would harden his heart to it, it's what he always did. He was a master at it.

He had to say goodbye to Rosalind Sutton, once and for all.

Rosalind awoke to the soft creak of a door. She opened her eyes just in time to see Griffith closing the door.

"Good morning."

She smiled at him as she brushed her curls out of her face. The sheet fell to her waist as she sat up and bared her breasts to his gaze. A touch of shyness still persisted. But the pleasant drowsiness that lingered in her limbs made her confident as she threw back the covers and walked to him.

"You're up early."

She went up on her toes and brushed a kiss across his lips. He didn't reciprocate.

He grabbed her by her arms and held her away from him.

She blinked as she saw the reservation in his eyes.

"Are you okay?"

"I have something for you."

She smiled and let one hand drift down his chest. "If it's what I'm thinking—"

He caught her wrist, stopped her exploration. "It's not."

Stung by his dismissal, she took a step back. Worry pooled in her stomach.

"Griffith, what's wrong?"

He picked up an envelope from a nearby table. He'd clearly brought it into the room with him. Cold slithered up her spine as her fingers closed over the packet.

"I signed it this morning."

"I thought..."

She stared down at the envelope, at his name written at the top and the date she'd received her assignment. Over a month and a half ago. How had she gone from despising the man in front of her to…

*To what? Sleeping with him?*

"I thought you weren't ready."

"I'll never be ready. You helped me see that."

Alarm bells still clanged. He wasn't the same Griffith Lykaois she'd met when she'd first ended up stranded at the chateau. But the camaraderie they had developed over the past week, not to mention the intimacy they'd shared over the past couple of days, had disappeared.

"There's a crew working on the bridge."

He said it so casually it took a moment to penetrate. When it did, the relief and happiness she'd expected didn't surface. No, it was disappointment.

"Oh."

"Beatrice tried to come up this morning and saw the tree blocking the bridge. She sent a crew from the village to remove the tree."

"And the bridge?"

"So far it looks all right. I was able to make a call. An inspector is arriving this afternoon and will confirm if it's safe to drive on." His expression remained placid. "But given that half a dozen men were on it this morning, it appears safe to walk across."

She forced a smile. "That's great."

"I've arranged for you to fly back to London on my private jet. There's an airfield near here—"

"Wait." Her head spun. She held up a hand. "You just… you made all of these plans? Without even talking to me?"

"Your boss will be pleased." He gestured to the envelope. "The documents are signed. You can go back to London and present this to your superiors. It's what you wanted."

"It was. It is." She stood. Suddenly conscious of her nudity, she moved to the bed and grabbed a shirt he'd thrown on the footstool the night before, hastily buttoning it up to cover herself before she turned to face him again. "But what about us?"

The sigh he released tied her stomach into knots so tight she could barely breathe.

"Rosalind."

He said her name so gently, as if he were talking to a child. Before he could continue, she turned away.

"I see."

She'd known this was a risk. Had accepted it when she'd decided to take the leap and share her body with Griffith. How many times had she fought her attraction, told herself that she shouldn't let herself get carried away?

The sight of the ocean waves rising and falling drew her to the windows. She crossed her arms over her chest, watched the familiar sight with a desperation that made her feel weak, fanciful.

Foolish.

She'd let her body rule, let her heart take the lead, instead of listening to her brain, to her instincts warning that while she might thoroughly enjoy her time with Griffith, he would ultimately break her heart.

"Rosalind," he said again. "We talked about this. About the differences between us and what we want."

"I know." She sucked in a steadying breath, reached for an inner strength that eluded her. "I just…" No matter what he'd said, she knew something had shifted between them. Knew what had started as pure sex, pure hedonistic enjoyment, had morphed into something else.

Her voice trailed off as her mind raced. Did she tell him what was in her heart? What she had realized last night as they'd made love under the stars?

That she had fallen in love?

It was too much too soon, she knew. Especially to be in love with a man who believed himself incapable it. A man who hid behind this monster persona to keep himself protected from the grief life inevitably threw in one's path.

Yet hadn't she dealt with her own grief in an unhealthy way? Pursuing a career that, from the beginning, she'd had misgivings about? All in some misguided way of honoring her mother's memory when she knew, deep in her heart, that her mother would have been devastated if she would have realized how unhappy her daughter had become.

Yes, Griffith had work to do. So did she. Didn't everyone? But behind the hurt was the man she'd glimpsed, the one who had cared for her, loved her body, taken her on a walk to calm her mind, encouraged her to follow her dreams…

"Will we see each other again?" One hand fluttered in the air between them. "Obviously I don't have much to go on, but this, what happened between us…that meant something to me."

"It meant something to me, too."

He said the words, but the lack of inflection, the flat tone, said differently, twisted the knife in her heart.

"We could—"

"I can't give you what you want, Rosalind." Suddenly Griffith stood before her, eyes glittering with pain and anger. "Not because I don't want to, but because I can't. I will inevitably mess up. If I couldn't be the kind of son my father deserved, what makes you think I could even come close to being the kind of man worthy of you?"

"Do you even believe half the things you tell yourself?"

He blinked. "Excuse me?"

"You told me you weren't the same after your mother's passing. Everyone responds to grief differently. Would it have wrecked you so much if you hadn't cared about her? What about your father? Would you be this upset, this wrecked, if you didn't love him? The company you work so hard for, the one you never let down even when you were spending like crazy and dating slews of women?"

"Obviously I didn't care enough. If I had, I wouldn't have kept my father at a distance until it was too late."

The words hung in the air between them, wiped away her moment of anger as pain surged forth. She started forward, to lay a comforting hand on his arm, to soothe away his anger and fears.

But once again he moved out of her reach, quelled her motion with a single glare that gave her a glimpse of the reputation that had supposedly made grown men quake in the boardroom.

"I know that I can't offer you what you want, Rosalind. We can't all live our lives with such an overly optimistic outlook. Us. Your career."

"My career?"

"Yes, your career. You're continuing with this charade that you want to reach the next level with a prestigious firm instead of examining your life and deciding what you really want."

Anger punched through the hurt.

At a loss for words, she turned away, ran her hands through her hair as she tried to think, tried to make sense of the jumble of thoughts clamoring for space inside her head. Pain took front and center, that he would be so dismissive of her feelings, of what they had shared. Yet hadn't he told her, repeatedly, he was too selfish to engage in anything beyond what little time they had been given? Had she been so captivated by their physical chemistry that she had let herself mistake attraction for something more?

Doubt hovered at the edges of her pain. She wondered if she had let herself be swept up in the romance of her first lover, in the novelty of their glamorous seclusion, instead of seeing things for what they were.

And now doubt that she was even capable of separating fantasy from reality. Even before she'd set foot inside Chateau du Bellerose, she'd questioned her future with Nettleton & Thompson. But she'd brushed aside her misgivings, focusing on living as much as she could, on achieving the loftiest goals, to do her mother proud.

She swallowed hard before turning back to face Griffith.

"You make a good point." He blinked, as if she'd surprised him. "And that is something I'll have to deal with. Sometimes people don't respond the way that they should to loss," she added quietly. "I don't think either of us dealt with our grief in a good way. It doesn't mean that's the way we have to stay."

"No, it doesn't."

He let out a shuddering breath. Closed his eyes. When he opened them, she saw his answer in his eyes.

And it broke her heart.

She moved then, walking toward him with an outward confidence she didn't feel. She reached up, ignoring the barely perceptible flinch as she laid her hands on his cheeks.

"I do sometimes look at things unrealistically. With too much optimism. Sometimes I do exactly as you suggest and turn a situation into a positive when actually it sucks and needs to be fixed. Sometimes I avoid discomfort." She blinked rapidly, willed herself not to cry. "But isn't that better than embracing misery. Not allowing yourself to feel anything else."

He tried to step back. She held on for just a moment, leaned up on her toes and gently kissed the scar that cut over his cheekbone. His sharp intake of breath nearly undid her as she pulled away.

"I think what's truly the saddest of all," she said as she moved to the door, "is that you can't see yourself as I do."

"With rose-colored glasses?"

"No." She glanced back over her shoulder. He stood, framed in the morning light, body tense and poised as if he would run away at any moment. "As someone who made mistakes, realized he made mistakes and is trying not to repeat them. You're not perfect, Griffith, and you never will be. And maybe you will never want what I want out of life. But that doesn't mean you can't be someone you could be proud of. Someone who does good with all of his money and influence."

"Or perhaps," he said, his voice low and bordering on a growl, "I'm exactly the man I told you I am and you're just not listening."

She nodded toward the gilded mirror on the wall, the one they'd stood in front of last night as he'd undressed her, worshipping her body with such care it had warmed both her body and her soul.

"Take a good long look at yourself, Griffith. I hope one day you'll realize you're the only one who sees yourself as a monster."

With that final pronouncement, she grabbed the signed contract that she'd come here for all those days ago, stepped out into the hall and closed the door.

# CHAPTER FIFTEEN

"CONGRATULATIONS, ROSALIND."

Rosalind blinked and refocused on the couple seated on the opposite side of the massive walnut desk.

"Thank you."

Mr. Robert T. Nettleton nodded, his smile wide and bright. At sixty-three he was still an attractive man. His silver hair was cut just long enough to be combed back from a broad forehead touched with only the faintest wrinkles that made him look distinguished rather than old.

Ms. Kimberly Thompson sat to his right. Sharp angles and a strong jaw went against traditional standards of beauty. But it was an arresting face that, coupled with her quiet confidence and *Mona Lisa* smile, made one look twice.

Nettleton slid the signed contract out of the envelope. His smile broadened as he stared down at Griffith's signature. Rosalind waited for a sense of victory, of accomplishment.

Nothing. Nothing but the persistent numbness that had settled over her like a shield when she'd walked away from Griffith's room.

"You've always been an asset to this firm, Rosalind."

*Really? Even when you threatened to fire me?*

"Thank you, sir."

"Which is why we'd like to offer you the position of midlevel attorney."

His words washed over her. The words she had been working toward for the past two years.

In a flash, she saw the next five years. No weekend jaunts to Europe as she worked longer hours. The couple of trips she took home every year becoming fewer and further between even though she would be making more money to cover the cost.

No pleasurable afternoons reading on a patio. Indulging in a sun-drenched picnic.

It hit her all at once.

*This isn't what Mom wanted. She wanted you to do what made you happy. She thought this would, that's why she pushed you so hard. She wanted you to have the financial security to do whatever you wanted. Whatever made you happy. To have options.*

"Rosalind?"

She looked up to see Nettleton watching her, the smile still in place but a faint crinkle between his brows.

"Sorry, sir." She shook her head. "I just…"

Temptation flared, bright and blinding for one spellbinding moment. To take the safe choice.

And then it disappeared. Where had it gotten her before? Lonely. Overworked. Heartbroken.

"This is what I thought I wanted. But recently, I've come to realize that I've been trying to be someone I'm not."

Robert sputtered. "You're quitting."

"Yes." Rosalind smiled. "Yes, sir, I'm submitting my notice."

"You can't just quit the most prestigious—"

Kimberly silenced her colleague. She gave Rosalind a slight smile before shooting Robert a cold gaze that made his continued objections fall silent. "What will you do now?"

"Take a break. Go to Maine and visit my family." She glanced out the window at the clouds scuttling over the London skyline. Even on stormy days, England had become home. "Then come back and start my own firm."

Kimberly blinked. And then she smiled, a true smile that stretched from ear to ear.

"It'll be a lot of work."

Robert muttered something under his breath, but Rosalind ignored it.

"It will be. But I'll get to work with the kind of clients that got me interested in doing this." She grinned. "And I'll get to call the shots."

She walked out of the office with her head held high. Each step she took buoyed her confidence, until she was fairly brimming with it.

Was she scared of the uncertainty, worried about what the next phase of life had in store for her? Absolutely. But she would get to tackle it on her own terms with her own dreams leading the way.

She should call her father. Tell him she was coming home for a visit. Tell him in person about the momentous decision she had made.

*Two weeks.*

Two weeks and she'd be free. Free to take on the next phase of her life on her own terms.

She reached into her pocket for her phone. Her fingers brushed something smooth and cool. Her heart twisted as her hand closed around the small white stone Griffith had given her on their walk. She'd nearly left it behind but at the last second had tucked it into her pocket when she'd changed back into the clothes she'd worn to the chateau. Then forgotten about it as she'd drifted through a haze of heartache as she'd traveled back to England.

She pulled it out now, let it lay flat on her palm. The man could have bought her rare paintings, diamonds, a private jet.

But the rock, a simple token that had made him think of her, meant more to her than anything else in the world he could have bestowed upon her. The urge to call him, to tell him he had been right, that she had finally broken free and decided to take the risk of being herself, nearly won out.

Until she remembered his face when she had walked away. The cold hardness in his eyes, the resoluteness in his clenched hands. She truly hoped he would find peace. Would come to terms with who he was and who he could be.

But he wasn't ready. Not for his past and not for his future. Which meant he wasn't, and might not ever be, ready for her. Self-doubt had her wondering if she wasn't enough, if her love wasn't enough.

Except she knew it had nothing to do with how much she loved him, even if she hadn't told him so directly. Until he could accept himself, love himself, nothing would ever be enough.

Sadness wrapped bitter fingers around her heart and squeezed. She clenched her eyes shut, let herself experience the grief for a heartbeat.

Then pushed it away. Now was not the time for mourning.

She tucked it into her pocket before continuing on to her desk. Nostalgia hit, memories flickering through her like an old movie reel. The plant on the corner of her desk, the first thing she'd added on her first day. Meeting her first client as an associate attorney. Calling her parents after her first win in court.

Her lips curved into a sentimental smile. She wouldn't regret her time here. But in two weeks, when she would walk out of Nettleton & Thompson for the last time, she would be looking to her future.

Griffith stared out the window at the London Eye. The massive structure, white against the deep blue of a summer sky, slowly rotated. He'd ridden it plenty of times before, had even reserved a luxury dinner for an actress he'd enjoyed a weekend fling with.

But now, as he watched it turn, all he could think about was Rosalind and the ride she'd never gotten to share with her mother.

In the first few hours after she left, he had managed to focus on business, returning to the reports he had neglected in the days they had indulged in their brief but wild affair. But when he'd slipped into his bed that night, her scent had assailed him, drifted up off the pillowcase and summoned memories of her body wrapped around him as he'd driven himself deep inside her.

He'd ended up in a barren guest room on the second floor. But even glancing at the window as he'd fallen asleep, seeing the moonlight stream through the glass, had reminded him of her naked body awash in silver as she waited for him on the balcony.

Realizing that almost every room held some memory of her now, he'd made arrangements to leave for London the following day, walking across the bridge and to the edge of the road where he managed to get enough of a signal to reserve his private jet. It had been then that he had learned Rosalind had never shown up for her flight the day before. She must have purchased her own ticket back to England. It had stung, even if he understood why she had done it. Admired her for it.

He had known their separation would be painful. Had mentally prepared himself for it.

But no amount of preparation had kept him safe from the constant barrage of memories: a sip of wine on the plane reminding him of their cliffside picnic; the site of a rosebush making him think of the tender way she had stroked the rose petals in the garden, and her slow smile as if she had realized for the first time there was more to life than work, more than chasing after others' dreams instead of her own.

Time, he told himself. He just needed time. His relationship with Kacey had been his longest to date. But his time with Rosalind had been the most emotional, the most he'd ever allowed himself to get involved.

A few days had felt like a lifetime of knowing her. Of course, it would take time to let go.

Except instead of getting better, it was only getting worse.

He managed to get through the days. He returned to the office a week after arriving back in London. The meeting with his executive board had gone better than he had anticipated, with only a couple casting curious glances at his scars. A few of the staff members had had stronger reactions to his new face. Widened eyes, quickly looking somewhere else, even a gasp from an intern. He'd mostly ignored it, and in the case of the intern, had surprise himself by offering the young woman a slight smile and a comment of *It is a little jarring when you see it for the first time.* She'd stammered out a quick apology. Then they'd moved on.

It had been a little strange to discover that he had missed the daily interactions that came with being in the office. He'd been steeped in grief and isolation so long that he hadn't realized how much he enjoyed casual greetings, small talk with his secretary and the myriad of meetings that filled his day.

The nights, however, were hell. It was at night, in his penthouse in Knightsbridge, where his mind inevitably turned to Rosalind. What was she doing? Who was she with? And, the most pervasive: Was she happy?

Three weeks after she had walked down the drive and out of his life, he'd received a call from Mr. Nettleton directly, thanking him again for working with the firm and offering to represent Griffith's estate as the firm had represented his father's. Griffith had agreed to a meeting, surprising Nettleton when he had declined the attorney's offer to come to him and instead making the trip down to the law firm. It had been there that Griffith had discovered Rosalind had quit.

Even as he silently cursed Rosalind's decision to leave, mourned the chance to see her one last time, pride surged inside him. Whether she had taken his words to heart or discovered what she'd needed to make the decision on her own, she'd done more in the three weeks they'd been apart than he'd done in over a year. She'd taken charge of her life, made some hard decisions and moved on.

And what would he have done with that last meeting anyway? Apologize for how he'd ended things? He'd thought it would be the pain in her eyes that would haunt his dreams. The stricken look on her beautiful face when he'd taken the special moments they'd shared and ended them, swiftly and ruthlessly.

Except it hadn't been the pain. No, it had been that one aching moment when she'd looked at him with unabashed longing and resignation.

*You're the only one who sees yourself as a monster.*

A knock sounded on his door.

"Come in."

Alicia Hunter walked in. Even though she was nearly sixty, Alicia still commanded attention whenever she walked into a room, including the executive board she had served on for over thirty years, most recently as chair. From her trademark pant suits in vivid, jewel-toned colors to her short cap of silver hair that showcased her smooth dark skin and polished cheekbones to perfection. Her leadership and knowledge of shipping were legendary but so was her signature style.

That she had also played hide-and-seek with him when his father had brought him to the office as a child had added an amusing touch to their working relationship.

"Welcome back, Griffith."

"Thank you."

She tilted her head to one side. "You look good."

He arched a brow. "Really?"

"Yes." Her eyes narrowed as her gaze swept him from head to toe, assessing with a touch of maternal warmth. "Word is you're actually talking to people."

"I talked with people before."

"Not like this. You were always respected around here."

"But not particularly well-liked."

She shrugged. "It wasn't a matter of liking. You just

didn't do much to get to know the people who worked for you."

Because he had been focused on other things. Namely himself.

"Something I'm working on."

"It suits you." She moved to his desk and set her tablet down so he could read the screen. "The press conference is in twenty minutes. Daniel and I will be onstage with you," she said, referencing the chair of the board of directors.

"Good."

The public relations department had recommended a formal press conference to announce Griffith's official acceptance of his position as CEO of Lykaois Shipping after returning from his sabbatical. An event made more crucial after the media circus following Kacey's interview.

He'd known that something like this would be coming, had resisted the idea almost as much as he had resisted signing the contract accepting his inheritance. But now, as he glanced back out over London, he felt something deeper. Determination.

He'd experienced an unexpected sense of homecoming when he'd walked into the lobby on his first day back. He'd wondered if his emotional investment in Lykaois Shipping would change once he was surrounded by people again, by the company that bore his father's mark everywhere he looked.

Thankfully, he'd discovered that while there were still currents of grief and regret beneath the surface, they didn't weaken his resolve or his feelings. He did care about this company. *His* company. The people who worked for it. The legacy his father and grandfather had crafted.

As he'd assimilated back into the environment over the

past few weeks, his determination had only grown. On the few occasions he had experienced uncertainty, he'd squelched it. He could, as Rosalind had said, wallow in his own fears and misery. Or he could do something about it. And at least with the company, there were tangible measures of success he could look to, numbers and reports to create a foundation he could build from.

He slid some written notes over to Alicia. "Thoughts? Public Relations approved it. But I'd appreciate your eyes on it."

She picked up the paper, read through it quickly. "It's good."

"But?"

"You don't talk about your father a lot."

He looked down at his desk, splayed his fingers across the surface. The same desk his father had worked from. His grandfather before him. Months ago, the significance would have been lost on him. But now he recognized it for what it was, the meaning embedded in the faint scars, the streaks in the polished wood.

If he applied himself enough, focused on the company instead of himself, he would be at least half the leader his father had been.

"I don't think he would care for being included in any speech of mine."

The silence felt thick, heavy. His eyes flickered up to find Alicia watching him.

"What a thing to say."

Anger shimmered through him.

"Excuse me?"

"He was proud of you, Griffith."

He barked out a harsh laugh. "Yes. Proud of his over-indulgent son."

"He blamed himself."

Stunned, his head snapped up. "What?"

"Your father blamed himself for how you dealt with your mother's death." Alicia sighed, her shoulders drooping as if she'd been carrying a heavy burden for a long time and had finally let it go. "He told me that his family didn't talk much about their feelings. More of a soldier-on attitude."

Griffith remembered that well. He'd never doubted his father's love for him, for his mother. But he had overheard, more than once, his mother encouraging him to talk to her, to share the bad along with the good.

"I still made my choices."

"Yes. And he let you. He didn't try to talk to you, get you counseling, anything."

"I doubt I was in a place to listen."

"Eventually, no. But I remember those first few months, Griffith. You were obviously grieving and depressed. And Belen, as much as he loved you, didn't know what to do. He just assumed you'd buck up. By the time he realized how bad it was, you'd…found another way to cope."

*A delicate way to put it*, he thought in self-disgust.

"He loved you, Griffith. Even when you were at your most self-centered, you never let that bleed into your professional life. You accomplished a lot at a young age." The look she directed his way made him feel like he was five and had just been caught sneaking into the conference room to play with the projector. "Think. Do you really believe your father would have left you the fortune he did, or an international company, if he didn't think you were capable?"

Before he could reply to that astonishing bit of logic,

an assistant from the public relations department arrived to walk them down to the conference.

Minutes later Griffith was outside the front door of Lykaois Shipping, stationed behind a podium on an elevated stage as dozens of cameras flashed.

Instead of pushing the world away, retreating into his isolation, he stood and faced them.

He read his official statement. He paused at the end, took a breath.

"I hope to not only serve my employees and our clients, but to do my father proud." The improvised words, torn from his heart, were rough with emotion. "To honor the legacy my family has created."

Alicia placed her hand on his shoulder, squeezed. He acknowledged the gesture with a slight nod in her direction before turning his attention back to the reporters. Tried to stop looking for Rosalind amongst the sea of faces.

And failed.

He hadn't thought she'd be there. Why would she be? He'd pushed her away. Had told her in no uncertain terms they were done, that he didn't want to see her again.

Yet a foolish part of him had still hoped he would find her watching, encouraging him with that beautiful, confident smile of hers.

The first few questions were routine. Plans for future expansion, the exploration of adding a route through the Northwest Passage. One bold reporter asked about Kacey, a question Griffith deftly handled by arching a brow and replying with "I don't see what that has to do with shipping," much to the amusement of the others in attendance.

"Mr. Lykaois, what are you looking forward to in the coming year?"

His lips parted. Several answers would have been more than appropriate. But none of them felt right. None of them *were* right.

Because when he thought about the next year, his thoughts had nothing to do with Lykaois Shipping. They centered around a woman with unruly curls and a sunny smile who had fought her way through grief and still managed to find the good amidst the bad. Memories slipped into dreams of mornings spent on the patio of the chateau, afternoons exploring the neighborhoods of London he'd always avoided because they had never been wealthy enough to catch his interest. Dreams of a wedding, a ceremony that had never interested him but now made his heart twist at the thought of gazing down into her face and saying vows that would join them forever. And dreams of the life after: children, supporting Rosalind a she pursued her goals, hands joined through the ups and downs of life.

The crowd quieted. Whispers rippled through the crowd. Cameras clicked. The world watched as the answer became clear.

*Rosalind.*

He loved her. He loved her and he wanted to be with her. When he'd thought about the possibility of a future with her, it had been clouded by pain, by the habit of avoiding emotion for years, by his fear of hurting a woman who had seen the best in him even when he couldn't.

But when he stripped away all of that, when he answered the simple question with the simplest answer, it was Rosalind.

"There are several new initiatives we hope to focus on in the coming months. Some I can't speak to as the… details have not been hammered out yet. I will say that, as has been reported in the news, my father…" His voice caught. The lights flashed. "My father worked hard and, as I'm sure you've heard, left me with a substantial fortune. I'll be exploring ways to put that money to good use."

"No more champagne and caviar?" someone from the audience called out.

Griffith's chuckle cut through the mix of shocked murmurs and awkward laughter.

"Yes. But in moderation." He paused, then smiled. "Someone recently showed me there are more important things in life."

The questions came, fast and hard. He deflected, smiled as he stepped back from the microphone, ignoring the barrage of shouts as he allowed the assistant to guide him, Alicia and the other representatives from Lykaois Shipping back into the building.

It was only a few minutes later, even though it felt like hours, that he walked into his office and closed the door.

And finally confronted the realization that had nearly knocked him off his feet during the press conference.

*What happened between us...that meant something to me.*

His time with Rosalind had meant something to him, too. More than anything else in his life because he was in love with Rosalind. He loved her and wanted a life with her in it. Couldn't picture an existence without her in it.

And he'd forced her out of his life.

He quelled his panic, reined in his fear. Yes, she might reject him. That was her choice. But if he didn't ask the question, if he didn't tell her how he felt, what he wanted, he would never know.

He thought about calling, showing up at her flat.

*No.* Rosalind deserved something more. Something worthy of a fairy tale.

He picked up his phone, dialed his executive assistant. "I need you to make a reservation."

# CHAPTER SIXTEEN

ROSALIND STARED AT the cryptic invitation in her hand before her gaze moved to the towering white wheel in front of her. In all the years she'd lived in England, she had yet to ride the London Eye. It was one of the tallest Ferris wheels in the world and offered views of Buckingham Palace, Westminster Abby and Big Ben. One of the senior attorneys at Nettleton & Thompson had even been proposed to at the top of the wheel.

Another glance at the simple yet elegant card that had appeared in the mail a few days ago yielded few clues. The wheel normally closed at six o'clock. But her ticket indicated she should arrive at eight in the evening.

Her mind, along with her foolish heart, had immediately thought of Griffith, then dismissed him just as quickly. She'd heard nothing from him since they'd parted in France nearly five weeks ago. After her last day at Nettleton & Thompson, she'd gone home to Maine for a much-needed visit that had seemed to end almost as soon as it started. As she'd waited for her flight back to London, she'd given in to temptation and typed Griffith's name into her online search bar. An article had mentioned an upcoming press conference announcing Griffith assuming his father's role as CEO of Lykaois Shipping.

She'd been happy for him. But she'd also mourned that he had returned to England and made no attempt to see her.

*Just like he said he would.*

She breathed in deeply as she craned her neck back to look at the top of the Eye. Over thirty capsules with floor-to-ceiling windows were anchored to the wheel. At its height, the monument soared to well over four hundred feet. Her father and oldest brother, Jordan, had made plans to visit in the fall, and she planned to bring them here. Jordan would enjoy the ride while her father marveled over the engineering of the massive wheel.

A sentimental smile crossed her face as she approached the ticket booth. Her time in Maine had been not only a wonderful reprieve from the chaos of the previous weeks, but it had been a much-needed solace for her battered soul. She'd made more than one trip to the cemetery to lay flowers on her mother's grave. She'd also been surprised and relieved when her father had responded to news of her resignation and future plans with excitement and encouragement.

Part of her regretted the time she had spent chasing after something that had been tied to whom she thought she should be. Yet she couldn't regret the experience she'd gained, the people she'd met or how it had prepared her for the next step of operating her own firm. There would be long hours, yes, especially in the first year. But they would be spent doing what she loved. And as she grew, added to her staff and found success on her own terms, she would carve out time for the things she loved instead of just observing the good from afar.

Branches formed a leafy canopy overhead as she approached the main entrance. The queue lines were empty, the wheel immobile.

Frowning, she glanced down at the invitation again. It had come from the director of the Victoria and Albert Museum in Knightsbridge and suggested that she had been invited to a private ride on the Eye to discuss an upcoming exhibition. Believing it a prank, she'd called the museum directly. The director's secretary had assured her the invitation was genuine. The director, the young woman had shared, had heard that Rosalind was starting her own firm, and was actively recruiting up-and-coming London business owners to be a part of a new exhibition.

*Be a part of* was usually code for sponsorship. And while she'd saved up plenty of money working for Nettleton & Thompson and living in her tiny flat, the rent on the office space she'd decided on wasn't going to be cheap. Nestled between the neighborhood of Camden's vibrant market and social streets and its quieter residential area, it would be the perfect place to meet with the kind of clients she enjoyed working with.

Still, when the director of a world-famous museum sent her a private invitation, how could she say no?

Another glance at the ticket confirmed the date and time were correct. She'd suddenly realized that there was no one else there. Had she been the only one invited? Surely not. She looked around.

"Hello?"

"Good evening!"

A woman emerged at the top of the ramp leading up to the platform where guests boarded their capsule.

"Miss Sutton?"

"Yes."

"My apologies. I was getting your capsule ready. My name is Sara and I'll be your host this evening."

"It's nice to meet you."

"And you, ma'am. The rest of your party is ready."

"Oh. I'm sorry, I thought the invitation said eight o'clock."

"It did," Sara said with a reassuring smile. "The other guest arrived early."

Rosalind frowned. The museum secretary had made it sound like there would be a group of people, not just the director and her.

"Only one?"

"Yes, ma'am." Sara's eyes fairly sparkled. "This way."

Rosalind followed her onto the platform as she wracked her brain. She couldn't recall meeting the director before, or doing anything that would have drawn his attention.

"Here we are."

She looked inside the empty capsule. "There's no one else here."

"They'll be just a moment, ma'am."

Stifling a sigh, Rosalind walked inside and moved to the far side of the capsule. The water of the River Thames rippled as boats cruised by, from a long double-decker boat crowded with tourists to smaller sailboats that glided along the surface. The setting sun's rays turned the puffy clouds dotting the blue sky from white to shades of rosy pink and glowing orange.

Some of her uncertainty disappeared as she looked up once more. No matter what this meeting was actually about, at least the view from the top would be spectacular.

The wheel began to move, so slowly at first she almost didn't notice it. Surprised, she turned just as a man walked into the capsule.

Her heart began to pound in her chest, so fiercely she grasped one of the rails to steady herself.

"Griffith?"

"Hello, Rosalind."

Sara appeared in the doorway behind him, her face wreathed in an enormous smile. "Enjoy your ride!"

She shut and locked the door behind him, leaving Rosalind alone with the man she loved.

Griffith's eyes devoured the sight before him. Rosalind stood on the other side of the capsule, her chin lifted slightly, her eyes sharp and fixed on him. She'd regrettably pulled her hair into a loose chignon at the base of her neck. A few stubborn curls had managed to escape. The dress she'd worn, a simple sleeveless dress in forest green with a flared skirt and tantalizing V-neck, gave her a sense of class while mercilessly teasing him with a view of her long legs.

How had he gone over a month without seeing her? Without hearing her voice?

"Unless you took over as the director of the Victoria and Albert Museum, you owe me an explanation."

He bit back a smile at her tart tone. God, he'd missed her. She'd been one of the few people in his life to hold him accountable, to not let him get away with excuses.

He loved her for that.

"I may have made an arrangement with the director."

"May have?"

"Did," he admitted. "I did make an arrangement with the director. But," he added as she opened her mouth to interject, "it does involve a new exhibition. He just omitted that he would not be present at this first meeting."

She rubbed at her temples, as if staving off the beginnings of a headache.

"You could have just asked to see me, Griffith."

"Yes. But then I couldn't have surprised you."

She glanced over her shoulder as the capsule began its ascent. A small smile played over her lips.

"It is beautiful."

"I'm glad you like it."

When she turned back to face him, he had set the silver bucket he'd kept behind his back on the oval-shaped bench in the center of the capsule. The sound of her laughter, light and surprised, filled him as nothing else had since he'd left France.

"Champagne?"

"Yes. To celebrate the opening of the Victoria and Albert's new exhibition next spring."

He popped the cork and poured two glasses of bubbling golden liquid.

"What exhibition?"

He handed Rosalind her glass, savored her sudden inhale as their fingers brushed. Blood pumped through his veins at the sight of the blush that crept into her cheeks.

At the very least, she was still attracted to him. Perhaps he hadn't waited too long.

*"Recovery."*

Her brows drew together as one corner of her mouth kicked up into a confused smile.

*"Recovery?"*

"Artwork made by recovering alcoholics."

She paused with the glass halfway to her lips.

"What?"

"It's a form of therapy. I didn't know it existed until…"

He paused, tried to gather his thoughts as his heart started to pound. "Until I took someone's advice and started digging deeper into causes my parents cared about. Causes I could put more of myself into."

He turned away from her then. Even now, after everything that had happened the past two weeks, he still felt angry. Not as acute, but certainly persistent.

"One of the art schools my mother supported was trying to start up a therapy program for a clinic that treated alcoholics." His laugh was short, rough. "At first it felt like a cruel joke considering the accident. I wanted to walk away."

The soft rustle of fabric sounded behind him. He sucked in a breath a moment before she laid her hand on his back.

"But you didn't."

"No. I wanted to."

"My mother told me that doing the right thing when we didn't want to made it even more important."

"I would have liked to have met her."

"She would have liked you, too, Griffith."

He turned, caught her hand in his and brought it to his lips. He savored the flutter of her eyelashes as she looked down, the deepening of her blush.

"I'm working on believing that."

The smile she gave him nearly broke his heart. Sweet, kind, supportive. Fear kicked in, blazed bright for a moment.

And then he crushed it. Fear didn't have a place in this moment.

He kept his grip on her hand, led her to the bench and sat down. Their thighs brushed. His fingers tightened around hers as need built inside him. Not just a need for her body, but for her and everything that made up the incredible woman he'd fallen in love with.

"I listened to what the director of the program had to say. Why it was important. I agreed to a tour of the clinic."

Tears glimmered in her eyes. "Oh, Griffith."

"It was hard, Rosalind." He faced her, squared his shoulders as he surrendered control and shared his deepest fears. "It was even harder meeting the people who had made mistakes just like the man responsible for my father's death. To not redirect the anger I'd harbored toward myself onto them. But," he said quietly, "the clinic is trying to help them. So is the art school. And as someone reminded me, I could use some of my money to help make the world a better place."

"Griffith…" She reached up, laid her hand on his face as a tear slid down her cheek, followed by another as she dipped her head. "I can't… Saying I'm proud of you doesn't seem enough."

"It's enough. More than enough." He took her champagne glass from her and set them both down before grabbing her hands in his. "I love you."

Her eyes rounded as her lips parted.

"What?"

"I love you, Rosalind Sutton." He cupped her face, ran his thumb over the line of her cheek as he watched her. "I started to fall in love with you the moment I heard you bossing Lazlo around in his office."

She huffed. "I was not—"

He silenced her with a kiss. For one heart-stopping moment, she froze.

And then she bloomed in his arms, throwing her arms around his neck with abandon as she kissed him back. He groaned her name, thrilled to the sound of her answering moan. He pulled her onto his lap. Pressed her closer. Slid one hand into her glorious curls.

She pulled back, her arms still looped around his neck, her smile so bright and luminous it rivaled the sunset behind her.

"I love you, too."

His throat tightened. He leaned forward, rested his cheek against hers and breathed in her scent.

"I almost let you go. Almost let us go."

Her fingers moved across his back in soothing circles. "What made you come back?"

"I accepted my past for what it was and borrowed a page from your book by looking at how I could turn some of those traits into something good for the future." She started to say something, but he lay a gentle finger on her lips. "I'm afraid I'm going to fail myself. I'm not used to trying. To putting myself out there. Most of all," he admitted with a harsh exhale, "I worry that I'll fail you. That the man you think I can be won't stand the test of time."

"Oh, Griffith." She rested her forehead against his. "You'll make mistakes. I will, too. I made my own. I quit Nettleton & Thompson because you helped me realize that I was trying to be someone I wasn't. You showed me how to live. How to take joy from the simple things. How to make myself a priority instead of only living for others."

His arms tightened around her. "You deserve a life you love, Rosalind. Although I do appreciate your optimistic outlook." He leaned down, brushed a kiss across her temple. "You saw the potential in me when I couldn't."

"I do like looking at the sunny side of things and thinking hard work can solve anything." She let out a slow breath. "But it can't always be that way. You ground me."

"Just as long as I don't stop you from dreaming."

"No." Her smile took his breath away. "You encouraged me to take my own risk. To go after what I truly wanted and what I'm good at. For all my talk about looking at the sunny things in life, I wasn't letting myself live."

"I'm glad. And I'm proud." Surprisingly, his next admission was the hardest one to make. "The exhibition…"

"Oh!" She laughed, snuggled into his embrace. "I completely forgot. Tell me everything."

"When I dropped by last week, they gave me a tour of the studio. Right now, it's just a spare room, but come spring they'll have a new addition to the clinic." He smiled slightly. "There was an older woman in the back corner of the room when I visited. She wasn't done, but her canvas was partially covered by a field of flowers. Square ones, diamond-shaped, rectangles and all sorts of colors that shouldn't work. But they did. She told me how she started drinking after her husband passed away. How she was painting the field where he proposed and how the art helped her process her husband's death. Helped her stop drinking. It got me thinking. Maybe other people would like to see their artwork, too, hear their stories. That maybe I could do more to help. *Recovery* will open with featured artwork from members of the clinic's art therapy program. Admission fees will fund treatment. Artists can be anonymous, but most are sharing their names. They have the option of keeping their work when it's over, or having it auctioned off at a gala to celebrate the end of the exhibition."

"Griffith…" Her tremulous smile made his blood sing.

"It's a step. Maybe one day I'll be able to forgive the man who hit my car. Forgive myself for all the years I wasted not dealing with my mother's death."

"You don't have to do it alone."

He slipped an arm under her legs and the other behind her back as he lifted her up, held her tight for a moment and then set her on the bench next to him. Before she could move, he slid off the bench and got down on one knee.

Her eyes widened. "Griffith..."

"You make me want to be a better man, Rosalind. You make me want to be the best I can be. And while I'm terrified I will let you down, I want to try. I want to go to bed with you every night and wake up to you every morning. I want to hear your thoughts, live with you in our chateau by the sea with five or six kids running around."

"Six?" she asked with a laugh. "How about three?"

"Four." He kissed her again, simply because he could, and then reached into his jacket pocket. When he flipped the lid open on the white velvet box, she gasped.

"This was my mother's." The yellow pear-shaped diamond winked up at them, set on a gleaming silver band and surrounded by smaller jewels. "Rosalind, would you do me the honor of becoming my wife?"

The words had barely left his lips when she flung her arms around him.

"Yes! Yes, Griffith!"

Laughing, he pulled back long enough to slide the ring onto her finger before sweeping her into his arms and carrying her to the far side of the capsule. The sun hovered just above the horizon. The timeless landmarks of London, from the sprawling walls of the Houses of Parliament to the dome of St. Paul's Cathedral, lay below them.

He set her on her feet and pulled her snugly into his side.

"We missed almost the entire ride to the top."

Rosalind held out her hand, the ring glinting in the evening light.

"I'm not disappointed."

He cut her laugh off with another kiss.

"How soon will you marry me?"

"As soon as you want me to."

"I can bribe a justice as soon as we reach the bottom," he said. Then, seeing her pointed look, laughed and said, "All right, a week?"

"How about long enough for me to plan my dream wedding?"

"You don't already have it planned?" he teased.

She smiled up at him. "Bits and pieces. But I was missing the most important part. Until you."

# EPILOGUE

ROSALIND SIGHED AND wiggled deeper into the embrace of the plush egg chair in the garden. Spring had finally come to France, ushering in warm temperatures and budding blooms. Exhaustion and a vague sense of nausea had kept her inside the past week. But when she'd seen the green in the rose garden, heard the faint whistle of a bird outside her window, she hadn't been able to resist going outside.

She had nearly fallen asleep when a shadow fell across her. She opened her eyes and smiled when she saw her husband standing above her with a cup of tea in hand.

"Hello."

"Hello." He leaned down, kissing her warmly before pressing the mug into her hands. "You looked like you could use this."

"Thank you." She stifled a yawn as she noticed the package in his hands. "Did it come already?"

"Delivered by Beatrice and Jean this morning. Would you like to unwrap it?"

She laid a hand over his. "Thank you. But I think you should."

He nodded once, breathed in deeply and set about unwrapping the brown paper package tied up with string.

"Griffith…" She stared at the painting in his hands. "It's beautiful."

A sandy beach glimmered beneath a blazing sun. White chalk cliffs stood guard, including a familiar-looking arch that plunged into the deep blue sea just off the coast. The waves had been textured with a palette knife so that they rose up, almost as if they were about to swell off the canvas. A couple stood on the beach holding hands.

"Mary did well." Griffith held it up. "In the library? What do you think?"

"Perfect."

Rosalind smiled. The woman Griffith had spoken to on his first tour of the studio had grown from acquaintance into friend over the months. Seeing Griffith support her through her recovery, from taking her out for coffee to accepting her invitation to stand by her side at the unveiling of the exhibition, had made her even prouder of how far her husband had come in such a short amount of time.

"How is she doing?"

"Good." He smiled, pride evident in his voice. "She's been sober for ten months. She's still in counseling, but she said they've made a lot of progress. If things continue this well, her daughter said she'd like Mary to move in later this summer. Her and her husband are talking about trying for a baby this fall and want Mary to be involved with her grandchild."

"That's wonderful."

"She's volunteering at the clinic on Thursdays, too."

Rosalind didn't bother to hold back her smile of contentment. The nine months since Griffith had proposed to her had been a whirlwind. They'd celebrated an October wedding in the rose garden of the chateau, with Griffith flying her father and brothers over for the ceremony. The designer whose clothes she'd worn during that incredible week they'd first spent together had custom designed her wedding gown. The full skirt was colored the same pale blush as the pink Hermosa roses that had bloomed just before their wedding ceremony. Sparkling beads and light blue flowers threaded as the skirt and the sleeve that had covered one arm. The other arm had been left bare, adding a touch of sexiness that had made her feel all the more beautiful as she'd walked down the makeshift aisle to Griffith.

He'd also made headlines in his role as CEO, from expanding Lykaois Shipping's routes to his generous contributions to clinics, treatment programs and volunteer organizations. His philanthropy, especially in light of his father's passing, had been lauded.

Few knew how much those first steps had cost Griffith, how hard it had been to start down the road to forgiveness. A road that hadn't been entirely smooth, either. The first time he'd opened a letter from the man who had crashed into his car, he'd only made it a couple paragraphs in before he'd tossed the letter on the table and gone out for a walk. It hadn't been until after Christmas that he'd managed to make it through a whole letter.

Progress was progress. A phrase she told him as often as he needed to hear it, especially when he vacillated between the raging emotions of loss and the expectations he now set for himself.

And, she thought to herself with a small smile, a phrase he repeated back to her as she worked to get her firm up and running. Griffith had repeatedly offered to finance it, everything from payroll to office supplies. She'd turned him down flat on the money. She had, grudgingly at first, accepted his offers to help in other ways, including painting the walls of her new space and filing all the necessary paperwork to get started. Old habits, including the need to prove herself, had been hard to break. Yet as the months passed and her client list grew, she had come to recognize his support as the strength it was instead of a weakness on her part.

"How much did you pay for it?" She nodded toward the painting.

"A gentleman never tells."

*Recovery* had been an astounding success, running through the month of March with record numbers of guests paying the extra price for admission. It had been so wildly popular the museum had extended it by four weeks and promised to bring it back with new paintings.

The silent auction, too, had netted incredible results, with many of the artists receiving thousands of dollars for their work.

He carried the painting inside and returned a moment later. She scooted over, making enough room for him to join her. He wrapped his arms around her and pulled her close.

"Feeling better?"

"Much." She let out a sigh. "It would be nice if Mary's daughter had a baby next year."

"It would."

"It would be close in age to ours."

"Yes…" His voice trailed off as his head whipped around. "What?"

She grabbed one of his hands and guided it to her stomach. His fingers spread across her shirt, his eyes wide, his face full of wonder and disbelief.

"We're…you're pregnant?"

"Yes." She laughed, giddy at the thought that she

was carrying their child. "I'm guessing a little over two months, although I don't know for sure—"

He cut her off with a kiss that made her heart sing.

"Rosalind." He leaned back, cupped her face in his hands. "We're going to be parents?"

"We're going to be parents."

He laughed then, deep and joyful.

"It's going to be wonderful."

"But occasionally hard," she added.

"Yes." He kissed her again. "But we'll do it together."

"Together." She smiled. "Forever."

\* \* \* \* \*

*Did* Stranded and Seduced *leave you craving more? Then dive headfirst into the other instalments in The Diamond Club series!*

Baby Worth Billions *by Lynne Graham*
Pregnant Princess Bride *by Caitlin Crews*
Greek's Forbidden Temptation *by Millie Adams*
Italian's Stolen Wife *by Lorraine Hall*
Heir Ultimatum *by Michelle Smart*
His Runaway Royal *by Clare Connelly*
Reclaimed with a Ring *by Louise Fuller*

*Available now!*